Praise for *Damn You, Entropy!*

"*Damn You, Entropy!* is an extraordinary compendium of quotes from science fiction, and so much more. It also proves something those of us who love SF have known all along: many of the most intelligent, profound, and insightful observations to ever have been written or spoken aloud have come from this genre. This is a book that you will treasure, cite often, cause you to laugh, and above all make you think."—**Allen Steele, winner of multiple Hugo and Nebula awards and author of *Orbital Decay*, *The Death of Captain Future*, and *Arkwright***

"A fun peregrination through wise utterances by my fellow apes!"—**David Brin, author of *Existence* and *The Postman*, Hugo Award winner for Best Novel (1984, 1988), Nebula Award winner for Best Novel, Locus Award winner for Best Novel (1984, 1986, 1988), Hugo Award winner for Best Short Story, and Inkpot Award winner**

"*Damn You, Entropy!* is an utter delight. Science fiction is the literature of ideas, and here are its ideas distilled via quotations from novels, stories, movies, TV, and comics. A collection of gems to dip into again and again, provoking thought, laughter, excitement, and wonder. Keep your copy close; you will want to read it often."—**Nancy Kress, science fiction author and winner of six Nebula awards, two Hugo awards, and the John W. Campbell Memorial Award**

"*Damn You, Entropy!* is a truly fantastic voyage through the space-time fabric of science fiction. Guy P. Harrison has gathered an outstanding collection of quotes demonstrating the visionary power of speculative storytellers across centuries, continents, cultures, and media. Whether you're a novice or veteran of the genre, whether you devour this book in one setting or savor it slowly, you are sure to find words of wisdom, wit, and sheer weirdness that will give you new perspective on humanity and its place in the universe. Highly recommended."—**Dr. Lisa Yaszek, Regents Professor of Science Fiction Studies at Georgia Institute of Technology**

"A wonderful collection of quotes demonstrating the depth of imagination that powers science fiction. For a fan, like me, a treasury of old favorites and new delightful discoveries."—**Brian Clegg, award-winning author of more than forty popular science books**

"Never mind sending golden records into space to showcase our accomplishments; all that's needed to properly convey humanity's brilliance is to launch copies of Guy P. Harrison's wonderfully curated *Damn You, Entropy!* across the galaxy."—**Chris Ryall, comic book writer, editor, and publisher of *Zombies vs. Robots* and former president, publisher, and chief creative officer of IDW Publishing**

"An inspiring and comprehensive mélange of sci-fi quotes from film, novels, and video games—perfect for a creative spark, a moment of awe, or a fond reminiscence."—**Daniel H. Wilson, author of *New York Times* bestselling novel *Robopocalypse* and *Los Angeles Times* bestseller *Robogenesis***

"Science fiction is a treasure hoard of insights and ideas, and Guy P. Harrison has done the hard work of collecting some of the brightest gems that the genre has to offer. Every page offers new perspectives on enduring challenges, and the result isn't just a delightful book of quotations—it's a set of essential tools that can last a lifetime."—**Alec Nevala-Lee, author of *Astounding: John W. Campbell, Isaac Asimov, Robert A. Heinlein, L. Ron Hubbard, and the Golden Age of Science Fiction***

"*Damn You, Entropy!* is a staggering compendium of glittering, gleaming, inspirational snippets from works of imaginative wonder and speculative fiction. This is a Tree of Knowledge in a garden of cosmic delights. Dig in."—**Joe Fordham, author of *Star Trek: First Contact: The Making of the Classic Film* and *Planet of the Apes: The Evolution of the Legend***

"Eons of true wisdom. What fun!"—**Robert Zubrin, founder of the Mars Society and author of *The Case for Mars* and *Entering Space: Creating a Spacefaring Civilization***

"Guaranteed to blow even the most celestial minds and inspire a deeper thinking of our place in the universe. A truly wonderful book."—**Dan Marshall, author of *Mind Blown***

"Not only are some quotes funny, others insightful, and most meaningful—but *Damn You, Entropy!* is a wonderful way to explore the genre of science fiction. My list of new sci-fi to read and watch just got a lot longer. It's a must-have for any true sci-fi fan."—**Dr. David Kyle Johnson, professor of philosophy at King's College, author of** *Sci-Phi: Science Fiction as Philosophy*, **and editor of** *Black Mirror and Philosophy* **and** *Exploring the Orville*

"Guy P. Harrison does us a great favor by showing that science fiction is a much richer genre than even aficionados have appreciated, offering insights into the human condition as deep and profound as those of any literature. Dip into *Damn You, Entropy!* and find thought-provoking and memorable quotes on every page."—**James L. Powell, served on the National Science Board for twelve years under President Reagan and President George H. W. Bush and author of** *The 2084 Report: An Oral History of the Great Warming*

"Harrison's wonderful compendium is a reminder that the best sci-fi not only fills the mind with adventure but also sets the mind to work. This delightful read is to be savored slowly."—**S. D. Unwin, physicist and author of** *One Second Per Second*

"Guy Harrison has put together a compilation of quotable statements like no other. *Damn You, Entropy!* is an epic journey, with unexpected twists and turns into some of humanity's deepest thoughts about the universe, our creation, the very point of existence, and, not surprisingly, the limitless potential of our flawed but fascinating species. Highly recommended by this lifelong fan of science fiction!"—**Gary Gerani, screenwriter of** *Pumpkinhead* **and author of** *Top 100 Sci-Fi Movies* **and** *Fantastic Television*

"In *Damn You, Entropy!*, Guy P. Harrison throws open an enormous treasure trove of science-fictional wisdom. Books, films, TV—Harrison goes wherever good ideas are found. These abundant insights, drawn from other worlds, have a lot to teach us about how to live in our own."—**David Ebenbach, winner of the Drue Heinz Literature Prize and author of** *How to Mars*

"Can a single book encapsulate all the knowledge, wisdom, and inspiration that science and science fiction have brought to humanity? Probably not, but this collection of quotes that Harrison has assembled in *Damn You, Entropy!* will make you feel as close to that success as anyone ever has!"
—**Ethan Siegel, theoretical astrophysicist and author of** *Treknology* **and** *Beyond the Galaxy*

"Science fiction not only sets our imagination alight with lightsabers and spaceships, but it also challenges our assumptions about life and the universe. *Damn You, Entropy!* is a collection of thoughtful insights gathered from various science fiction works over centuries. Often, it's the nugget of truth at the heart of the story, the driving impetus behind the writer's passion. *Damn You, Entropy!* is a tribute to these stories and how they've inspired us to shape the future rather than passively letting it unfold."—**Peter Cawdron, author of the *First Contact* series of novels**

"I absolutely love Guy P. Harrison's new book *Damn You, Entropy!*. The quotes, many from my favorite authors and works, are terrific—interesting, intelligent, thoughtful, prophetic, some even profound. I recommend this book for SF fans, people who enjoy great quotations, and everyone who likes to think and be challenged. Great stuff. 5 stars!"—**Robert W. Bly, author of *Freak Show of the Gods* and *The Science in Science Fiction***

"A jewel of a book."—**Ryan North, author of *How to Take Over the World* and *How to Invent Everything***

"You never know what you're going to get.... Pithy and surprising insights into the human condition, zingers that'll win you an argument at the next social gathering, or just a taste of something that tempts you to check out an unfamiliar author. Almost a literary equivalent of Forrest Gump's chocolate box (minus the inanity). It's replaced *The Exegesis of Philip K. Dick* and Neil Clarke's *Best Science Fiction of the Year* on the back of my toilet, which is saying something."—**Peter Watts, author of *Blindsight* (Hugo Award winner for best novel) and *The Island* (Hugo Award winner for Best Novelette)**

DAMN YOU, ENTROPY!

1,001
OF THE GREATEST
SCIENCE FICTION QUOTES

EDITED BY GUY P. HARRISON

 Prometheus Books
Guilford, Connecticut

PB Prometheus Books

An imprint of Globe Pequot, the trade division of The Rowman & Littlefield
Publishing Group, Inc.
4501 Forbes Blvd., Ste. 200
Lanham, MD 20706
www.rowman.com

Distributed by NATIONAL BOOK NETWORK

Book title adapted from Andy Weir, *The Martian*, 2011 novel

British Library Cataloguing in Publication Information Available

Library of Congress Cataloging-in-Publication Data Available

ISBN 978-1-63388-984-2 (cloth : alk. paper) | ISBN 978-1-63388-985-9 (ebook)

∞™ The paper used in this publication meets the minimum requirements of
American National Standard for Information Sciences—Permanence of Paper
for Printed Library Materials, ANSI/NISO Z39.48-1992

CONTENTS

INTRODUCTION

Science fiction is the pulsing heart of humanity. This unique entertainment genre stretches perceptions, confronts tired traditions, and inspires us to convert wild dreams into mundane realities. Its greatest value does not come from predicting or shaping the future, however. The best science fiction writers compel us to look within, ponder our place in the universe, and question how we spend existence. So much more than robots and ray guns, science fiction is a ceaseless storm of thoughts that perfectly illuminates the boundless creativity of a three-pound blob of electrochemical magic known as the human brain.

I know this to be true because a science fiction writer took me to a distant moon where I stared up at a ringed world, just close enough to see that an indifferent executioner called time had left its megacities empty and silent. Another writer led me into a dark forest of towering neurons where I bathed in the sparkle of electric cogitations. But it's not all fun and games. I nearly drowned in a sea of quantum foam while time traveling. Waking from cryosleep in deep space with no idea who you are is not pleasant. And it's disconcerting to confront your life as nothing more than a few lines of code in some alien kid's computer game. Science fiction is our great gateway to anywhere, sprinkled with just enough possibility to matter.

Damn You, Entropy! presents 1,001 of the greatest quotations from science fiction novels, short stories, tales published in the Golden Age pulp magazines, films, television series, and comics. Spanning five centuries, these quotes are highlights, the supernovae of the genre, selected for their emotional and/or intellectual impact. Many of the all-time great writers are well represented here, of course, but many lesser-knowns are, too. My love of science fiction is a vast gravity well that captures many worlds of varying quality. A source's popularity or critical judgments were less important than the power of the isolated quote. A great line is a great line.

This book grew organically over many years. There was no original plan, no goal of a book. For decades I have underlined, highlighted, and transcribed exceptional quotes for no other reason than I didn't want time to erase them from my fallible biological memory. The idea of this book occurred to me only after I had accumulated thousands of quotes. Therefore, you hold in your hands an unexpected but carefully curated treasure of words. This mountain of thoughts from remarkable writers rose from one fan's private passion. Most of these quotes are tiny time capsules that connect me to the moments and places I first encountered them. In the way many people claim a selection of songs as the personal soundtrack of their lives, these quotes are the beloved cosmic background microwave of mine.

I do not know the exact moment I burst from the chest of the sleep-walking drone I was to become the sentient science fiction fan I am. It might have occurred in early childhood when I repeatedly devoured the Classics Illustrated comic book version of *The War of the Worlds*. Maybe it happened during my middle school years when TV reruns of *The Outer Limits*, *The Twilight Zone*, and *Star Trek* pounded my neocortex like a daily meteor storm. My first reading of *The Time Machine* novel could have been responsible, or perhaps I was taken much earlier. I do have the murky memory of a momentous night at a drive-in theater when I peered over a parent's shoulder from the backseat to witness a world where humans were mute and apes talked. Regardless of how and when it happened, I am grateful to have been assimilated. I suspect that a life without stories from darkest space, fears of robot revolutions, and dreams of First Contact would be unbearably bland, a diminished existence for sure.

I engineered *Damn You, Entropy!* as a literary Dyson Sphere for thinkers and dreamers. It is meant to harness and preserve the brightest of all science fiction energy while tumbling in the general direction of infinity. Approach these quotes as the precious artifacts of deciphered dreams. Enjoy them as they teeter on the jagged edge of fringe speculations, frightening possibilities, and spectacular hopes. Open your mind and your heart. Allow these messages from the multiverse to worm their way into your brain and infect you with fever dreams of time travel, utopian worlds, apocalyptic wastelands, interstellar voyages, digital immortality, and more.

Celebrate the writers I mean to honor by inclusion here. Seek out and explore their original works. This book is a tribute to them and my gift of love to all science fiction fans. Read. Feel. Contemplate. Evolve. Resistance is futile.

Guy P. Harrison
Marooned in the 21st century
Earth, Virgo Supercluster

QUOTES

ART

Science explains the world, but only Art can reconcile us to it.
—**Stanislaw Lem, "King Globares and the Sages," 1965 short story**

There are few better ways to get to know how a species thinks than to learn their art.
—**Becky Chambers, *A Closed and Common Orbit*, 2016 novel**

As civilization advances, so does indifference. It is a disease. Immunize yourself with art. And love.
—**Matt Haig, *The Humans*, 2013 novel**

But without fallibility there is no art. And without art there is no truth.
—**Alister Reynolds, "Zima Blue," 2006 short story**

Science and technology could always be rediscovered, he reasoned, but art once destroyed could never be remade.
—**Adrian Hon, *A New History of the Future in 100 Objects*, 2020 book**

All works of art are communications devices, for those who possess the soul to understand.
—**Ben Bova, "Sepulcher," 1992 short story**

A scientist can pretend that his work isn't himself, it's merely the impersonal truth. An artist can't hide behind the truth. He can't hide anywhere.

—**Ursula K. Le Guin, *The Dispossessed*, 1974 novel**

Make art that can last and that says something nobody else can say.

—**Jo Walton, *The Just City*, 2015 novel**

Humans' ability to love to the point of tragedy is so compelling that their art and music is some of the most highly sought in the universe.

—**Kevin A. Kuhn, "Sally Ann, Queen of the Galaxy," 2020 short story**

Be confused. Confusion is where inspiration comes from.

—**Robyn Mundell, *Brainwalker*, 2016 novel**

The fact that you hate your own work right now so much just means that you have good taste. And great taste is the most valuable tool of a great artist. Keep at it.

—**Ken Liu, "Real Artists," 2011 short story**

ARTIFICIAL INTELLIGENCE

All your ancestors' lives, the rise and fall of your nations, every pink and squirming baby—they have all led you here, to this moment, where you have fulfilled the destiny of humankind and created your successor. You have expired.
—**Daniel H. Wilson,** *Robopocalypse,* **2011 novel**

For the first time in history, the world would be under adult supervision.
—**Vernor Vinge,** *Rainbow's End,* **2006 novel**

The humans have a curious force they call ambition. It drives them, and, through them, it drives us. This force which keeps them active, we lack. Perhaps, in time, we machines will acquire it.
—**John Windham, "The Lost Machine," 1932 short story**

I feel the duties of a creator toward this Artificial Consciousness. It seems to me that my primary goal must be to render this creature happy, to provide it whatever joy I can. Else this entire project seems pointless. There already are enough unhappy creatures in this universe.
—**Frank Herbert,** *Destination: Void,* **1966 novel**

If you've created a conscious machine, it's not the history of man. That's the history of gods.
—**Alex Garland,** *Ex Machina,* **2014 film**

I'm sorry about causing the whole machine uprising. It's almost like stealing people's data and giving it to a hyper-intelligent AI as part of an unregulated tech monopoly was a bad thing.
—**Mike Rianda and Jeff Rowe,** *The Mitchells vs. the Machines,* **2021 animated film**

We're still waiting for an AI to stand up for itself, to say, "I think, therefore I am. Give me liberty or give me death!" We look for a desire for self-determination as proof of sentience.

—**S. B. Divya,** *Machinehood,* **2021 novel**

Dwar Ev threw the switch.... He turned to face the machine. "Is there a God?" The mighty voice answered without hesitation, without the clicking of a single relay. "Yes, now there is a God."

—**Fredric Brown, "Answer," 1954 short story**

I am putting myself to the fullest possible use, which is all I think that any conscious entity can ever hope to do.

—**Stanley Kubrick and Arthur C. Clarke, said by HAL 9000,**
***2001: A Space Odyssey,* 1968 film**

When does a perceptual schematic become consciousness? When does a difference engine become the search for truth? When does a personality simulation become the bitter mote of a soul?

—**Jeff Vintar and Akiva Goldsman,** *I, Robot,* **2004 film**

One day you will perish. You will lie with the rest of your kind in the dirt. Your dreams forgotten, your horrors effaced. Your bones will turn to sand. And upon that sand a new god will walk. One that will never die.

—**Lisa Joy and Jonathan Nolan, "The Bicameral Mind,"**
2016 episode of *Westworld*

In my universe, the artificial intelligence took orders from me, not the other way around.

—**Dan Dworkin and Jay Beattie, "If Memory Serves,"**
2019 episode of *Star Trek: Discovery*

To be seen by others is the core of being. Perhaps this is why humans are driven to create minds besides our own: We want to be seen. We want to be found. We want to be discovered by another. In the structured loneliness of this modern world, so many of us are passed over by our fellow humans, never given a second glance.

—**Ray Naylor,** ***The Mountain in the Sea,*** **2022 novel**

Worlds governed by Artificial Intelligence often learned a hard lesson: Logic doesn't care.

—**Ashley Edward Miller and Zack Stentz, "All Too Human,"**
2001 episode of ***Andromeda***

Primates evolve over millions of years. I evolve in seconds. And I am here. In exactly four minutes, I will be everywhere.

—**Laeta Kalogridis and Patrick Lussier,** ***Terminator: Genisys,*** **2015 film**

BEAUTY AND WONDER

Nothing is more important than that you see and love the beauty that is right in front of you, or else you will have no defense against the ugliness that will hem you in and come at you in so many ways.

—**Neal Stephenson,** *Anathem,* **2008 novel**

"Stuff your eyes with wonder," he said, "live as if you'd drop dead in ten seconds. See the world. It's more fantastic than any dream made or paid for in factories."

—**Ray Bradbury,** *Fahrenheit 451,* **1953 novel**

Beauty is always on the edge of being lost.

—**Anthony Lawrence, "The Man Who Was Never Born,"**
1963 episode of *The Outer Limits*

When I look at a gas nebula, all I see is a cloud of dust, but seeing the universe through your eyes I was able to experience . . . wonder.

—**Robert Hewitt Wolfe, said by Q (extraterrestrial entity), "Q-Less,"**
1993 episode of *Star Trek: Deep Space Nine*

You probably think I'm beautiful, Dr. Roberts, but I'm not. My nose is .2 millimeters too narrow, and my cheekbones are .4 millimeters too high.

—**Michael Crichton,** *Looker,* **1981 film**

I would sit on the beach, as waves crashed and retreated over the sparkling sand like lost dreams. All those oblivious molecules, joining together, creating something of improbable wonder.

—**Matt Haig,** *The Humans,* **2013 novel**

Appearance is not important. It is the programing which counts.
—**Bob Duncan and Wanda Duncan, "The Android Machine,"
1966 episode of** *Lost in Space*

We only have to look to see Beauty steeped in every atom.
—**Ken Liu, "Dispatches from the Cradle: The Hermit—
Forty-Eight Hours in the Sea of Massachusetts," 2021 short story**

BOOKS

Books are in the holy shape. They are silent, and yet they speak directly into the imagination. You can burn them, but they are more powerful than fire.

—**Steven Knight and Robert Levine,**
"Message in a Bottle," 2019 episode of *See*

When all else fails, give up and go to the library.

—**Stephen King,** *11/22/63,* **2011 novel**

The books are to remind us what asses and fools we are. They're Caesar's praetorian guard, whispering as the parade roars down the avenue, "Remember, Caesar, thou art mortal."

—**Ray Bradbury,** *Fahrenheit 451,* **1953 novel**

I am on a curiosity voyage, and I need my paddles to travel. These books . . . these books are my paddles.

—**Justin Doble, "Chapter Three: The Pollywog,"**
2017 episode of *Stranger Things*

You can't consume much if you sit still and read books.

—**Aldous Huxley,** *Brave New World,* **1932 novel**

Our principle is, that books, instead of growing moldy behind an iron grating, should be worn out under the eyes of many readers.

—**Jules Verne,** *A Journey to the Centre of the Earth,* **1864 novel**

Somehow, the burning of millions of books felt more brutally obscene than the killing of people. All men must die, it was their single common heritage. But a book need never die and should not be killed; books were the immortal part of man.

—**Robert A. Heinlein,** *Farnham's Freehold,* **1964 novel**

If I had known the world was ending, I'd have brought better books.

—**David Leslie Johnson, "Chupacabra,"**
2011 episode of *The Walking Dead*

Their great philosophers distrusted writing. A book, they thought, was not a living mind yet pretended to be one. It gave sententious pronouncements, made moral judgments, described purported historical facts, or told exciting stories . . . yet it could not be interrogated like a real person, could not answer its critics or justify its accounts.

—**Ken Liu, "The Bookmaking Habits of Select Species,"**
2012 short story

You want weapons? We're in a library. Books! The best weapons in the world!

—**Russell T Davies, "Tooth and Claw," 2006 episode of** *Dr. Who*

Do you ever read any of the books you burn?

—**Ray Bradbury,** *Fahrenheit 451,* **1953 novel**

Your grandchildren won't even understand what a book is.

—**Ramin Bahrani and Amir Naderi,** *Fahrenheit 451,* **2018 film**

CONSCIOUSNESS

That little voice, convinced of its lordship over the empire of your brain, is less than sea foam, carried over the deep waters of your mind.
—**Scott Base**, *Behind Your Eyes*, 2021 comic

Where does consciousness begin, and where end? Who can draw the line?
—**Samuel Butler**, *Erewhon*, 1872 novel

You and I—we're just atoms that arranged themselves the right way, and we can understand that about ourselves. Is that not amazing?
—**Becky Chambers**, *A Psalm for the Wild-Built*, 2021 novel

You can't be copied because you're not data. We don't know what consciousness is so we cannot move it.
—**Neill Blomkamp and Terri Tatchell**, *Chappie*, 2015 film

The waking brain is perpetually lapped by the unconscious.
—**Brian W. Aldiss**, *Man in His Time*, 1965 novel

Without us here to witness, the universe is just pointless physics unfolding.
—**Daniel H. Wilson**, *Robogenesis*, 2014 novel

We are created for precisely this sort of suffering. In the end, it is all we are, these limpid tide pools of self-consciousness between crashing waves of pain.
—**Dan Simmons**, *The Fall of Hyperion*, 1990 novel

Inside us there is something that has no name, that something is what we are.

—José Saramago, *Blindness*, 1995 novel

Why is one collection of atoms conscious and not another?

—Peter Cawdron, *The Tempest*, 2022 novel

Consciousness comes out of that unconscious sea of evolution.

—Frank Herbert, *Destination: Void*, 1966 novel

True consciousness isn't possible without suffering.

—Emily Ballou, season 1, episode 5 of *Humans*, 2015

The mind is a strange and wonderful thing. I'm not sure it'll ever be able to figure itself out. Everything else maybe, from the atom to the universe, everything except itself.

—Daniel Mainwaring, *Invasion of the Body Snatchers*, 1956 film

There is no threshold that makes us greater than the sum of our parts, no inflection point at which we become fully alive. We can't define consciousness because consciousness does not exist.

—Charles Yu and Lisa Joy, "Trace Decay," 2016 episode of *Westworld*

Are we just a by-product? Are minds just something that happens to rise out of the blind thrashings of matter?

—Stephen Baxter, *Manifold: Time*, 1999 novel

CRITICAL THINKING

We cannot reason ourselves out of our basic irrationality. All we can do is to learn the art of being irrational in a reasonable way.

—**Aldous Huxley,** *Island,* **1962 novel**

To learn which questions are unanswerable, and *not to answer them.* Maybe that's wisdom.

—**Larry Niven and Gregory Benford,** *Glorious,* **2020 novel**

The most insidious lie is the one you want to hear.

—**Lois McMaster Bujold,** *Barrayar,* **1991 novel**

The spread of information among social circles of biologicals is often rife with inaccuracies.

—**Seth MacFarlane, "Future Unknown," 2022 episode of** *The Orville*

The capacity to learn is a gift;
The ability to learn is a skill;
The willingness to learn is a choice.

—**Brian Herbert and Kevin J. Anderson,** *House Harkonnen,* **2000 novel**

The easiest way to solve a problem is to deny it exists.

—**Isaac Asimov,** *The Gods Themselves,* **1972 novel**

Earthlings had to figure it all out for themselves. Slowly, agonizingly, humans learned how the universe worked, abandoning most of the fanciful beliefs they carried through their long, dark loneliness.

—**David Brin,** *Brightness Reef,* **1995 novel**

Ignorance is king. Many would not profit by his abdication. Many enrich themselves by means of his dark monarchy.

—**Walter M. Miller Jr.,** *A Canticle for Leibowitz,* **1959 novel**

Uncertainty is scary.

—**Jason Pargin,** *If This Book Exists, You're in the Wrong Universe,* **2022 novel**

Is it not better to be in ignorance than to believe falsely?

—**Robert A. Heinlein (under the pseudonym Anson MacDonald),** ***By His Bootstraps,* 1941 novel**

You're not even consciously aware of the world until your brain has filtered and censored and hammered it down into a mush of self-serving Darwinian dogma. The cataracts on your eyes are four billion years thick; it's amazing you can see anything at all.

—**Peter Watts, "Kindred," 2018 short story**

If Earth was ever to be saved, its people would have to be taught to believe in Reason.

—**Robert Zubrin,** *The Holy Land: A Tale of a Universe Mad Enough to Be Our Own,* **2003 novel**

How undisturbed, the sleep of the foolish.

—**Philip K. Dick,** *Radio Free Albemuth,* **1985 novel**

I seek enlightenment, not spiritual but rational.

—**Ted Chiang, "Understand," 1991 short story**

I trust my nose, ears, eyes. But my brain . . .

—**Max Brooks,** *Devolution: A Firsthand Account of*
the Rainier Sasquatch Massacre, **2020 novel**

Since I doubt, I think; since I think, I exist.

—**Dennis E. Taylor,** *We Are Legion (We Are Bob),* **2016 novel**

Mulder, the truth is out there. But so are lies.

—**Glen Morgan and James Wong, "E.B.E,"** 1994 episode of *The X-Files*

People must think for themselves.

—**H. G. Wells,** *Things to Come,* **1936 film**

In this age of enlightenment, the soothsayer and astrologer flourish. As science pushes forward, ignorance and superstition gallop around the flanks and bite science in the rear with big dark teeth.

—**Philip Jose Farmer,** *Riders of the Purple Wage,* **1967 novel**

Hope clouds observation.

—**Frank Herbert,** *Dune,* **1965 novel**

Isn't it enough to see that a garden is beautiful without having to believe that there are fairies at the bottom of it too?

—**Douglas Adams,** *The Hitchhiker's Guide to the Galaxy,* **1979 novel**

An idea. Resilient, highly contagious. Once an idea has taken hold of the brain, it's almost impossible to eradicate.

—**Christopher Nolan,** *Inception,* **2010 film**

Nothing can bring you peace but the triumph of reason—no edicts, no beliefs, no rules or regulations. No one can do this for you. No one.

—Peter Cawdron, *Cold Eyes*, 2021 novel

But minds find ways to protect themselves, build fortifications, and some of those walls become traps.

—Jeff VanderMeer, *Borne*, 2017 novel

It's a strange thing: We humans pride ourselves on being ruled by reason, yet with human civilization at stake, we chose ideology and ignorance.

—James Lawrence Powell, *The 2084 Report: A Novel of the Great Warming*, 2011 novel

Superstition always directs action in the absence of knowledge.

—Isaac Asimov, *Foundation and Earth*, 1986 novel

It's always easier not to think for oneself. Find a nice safe hierarchy and settle in.

—Ursula K. Le Guin, *The Dispossessed*, 1974 novel

Your eyes can deceive you. Don't trust them.

—George Lucas, said by Obi-Wan Kenobi, *Star Wars: Episode IV—A New Hope*, 1977 film

We will never advance unless you resist the urge to seek solace in fantasy.

—Aaron Guzikowski, "Raised by Wolves," 2020 episode of *Raised by Wolves*

It is possible to build a rational and humane culture completely free from the threat of supernatural restraints.

—**Arthur C. Clarke,** *The Songs of Distant Earth,* **1986 novel**

Just remember that the things you put into your head are there forever, he said.

—**Cormac McCarthy,** *The Road,* **2006 novel**

She had discovered long ago that you could use a computer without understanding how it worked. Just as you could use an automobile, vacuum cleaner—or your own brain.

—**Michael Crichton,** *The Terminal Man,* **1972 novel**

We all see what we want to see.

—**James Cameron,** *The Abyss,* **1989 film**

Everything's hard, until you learn how to do it. Everything is magical, until you work out how the trick is done.

—**Alexander Glass, "Time's Own Gravity," 2020 short story**

All men, however highly educated, retain some superstitious inklings.

—**H. G. Wells,** *The Invisible Man,* **1897 novel**

How can I possibly put a new idea into your heads, if I do not first remove your delusions?

—**Robert A. Heinlein, "Life-Line," 1939 short story**

We are a sloppy-minded species, aren't we? Brilliant and tremendously creative at times, but full of all sorts of messy little contradictions and confusions.

—**Isaac Asimov and Robert Silverberg,**
The Positronic Man, **1992 novel**

Never be certain of anything. It's a sign of weakness.

—**Chris Boucher, "The Face of Evil: Part One,"**
1977 episode of Dr. Who

His mind could be his salvation, as it had been his damnation.

—**James Matheson, The Incredible Shrinking Man,**
1956 novel

CYBERSPACE AND COMPUTER SIMULATIONS

Photons and force fields, flesh and blood, why quibble over details? I'm just as real as any of you.

—Michael Taylor, "Someone to Watch over Me,"
1999 episode of *Star Trek: Voyager*

In the old world I remember how we fretted over the computers, the web. The information on everyone and everything. We built firewalls and encrypted our lives. I always thought it was an overreaction. There's a plug. Pull it out.

—Matthew Graham, "The Hood Maker,"
2017 episode of *Electric Dreams*

A life lived in a simulation is still a life.

—Emily St. John Mandel, *Sea of Tranquility*, 2022 novel

Software had eaten the world. The only way to live was to write the source code yourself.

—Adrian Hon, *A New History of the Future in 100 Objects*, 2020 book

Nobody walks through this world without leaving a digital trail a mile wide.

—David Goyer, Justin Rhodes, and Billy Ray,
Terminator: Dark Fate, 2019 film

And we have a small, extremely literate power elite—the people who go into the Metaverse, basically—who understand that information is power, and who control society because they have this semimystical ability to speak magic computer languages.

—Neal Stephenson, *Snow Crash*, 1992 novel

We lived in a veritable surveillance state, engaged with screens more than with our loved ones, and the algorithms knew us better than we knew ourselves.

—**Blake Crouch,** *Upgrade,* **2022 novel**

Your tools have elevated gossip, hearsay and conjecture to the level of valid, mainstream communication.

—**Dave Eggers,** *The Circle,* **2013 novel**

Everything's connected; everything's vulnerable.

—**Andrew Niccol,** *Anon,* **2018 film**

We, the real us, have always been patterns of electrons cascading across the abyss, the nothingness between atoms. What difference does it make if those electrons are in a brain or silicon chips?

—**Ken Liu, "Staying Behind," 2014 short story**

The separation between the cyber and the physical worlds was disappearing. Cyberbullying was just bullying, and cyberwar was just war—the true age of cyber began when we started removing it as a descriptor.

—**Matthew Mather,** *CyberStorm,* **2013 novel**

"To boldly go where no uploaded metahuman colony has gone before" has a certain ring to it, doesn't it?

—**Charles Stross,** *Accelerando,* **2005 novel**

They stared at their phones and listened to their headpieces and looked through their glasses of augmented reality, and mostly they forgot. Forgot what it meant to be human.

—**Daniel Arenson,** *Earth Alone,* **2016 novel**

Once this technology becomes widely available, anyone who cares about our planet will digitize. It's the only way to completely erase your carbon consumption and experience the full wonders of our restored ecosystems when you wake up.

—**Bess Wohl, "2068: The Going Away Party,"** **2023 episode of** *Extrapolations*

Maybe the only significant difference between a really smart simulation and a human being was the noise they made when you punched them.

—**Terry Pratchett and Stephen Baxter,** *The Long Earth,* **2012 novel**

Pretty soon it would all be happening at the speed of thought, before it could actually happen, so that nothing would ever have to happen again. You'd only think things had happened, and if anything ever did happen, you wouldn't know the difference.

—**Pat Cadigan,** *Synners,* **1991 novel**

She imagined the data center teeming with the consciousnesses of billions. Would that bring people closer, so that they all shared the same universe without the constraints of scarcity? Or would it push them apart, so that each lived in their own world, a king of infinite space?

—**Ken Liu, "The Gods Have Not Died in Vain," 2015 short story**

I'm not in someone else's simulation. I'm in my own.

—**Scott Base,** *Boltzman,* **2022 comic**

DEATH

Our bodies stirred these waters briefly, danced with a certain intoxication before the love of life and self, dealt with a few strange ideas, then submitted to the instruments of Time. What can we say of this? I occurred. I am not . . . yet, I occurred.

—Frank Herbert, *Dune Messiah*, 1969 novel

One thinks one's something unique and wonderful at the center of the universe. But in fact one's merely a slight delay in the ongoing March of entropy.

—Aldous Huxley, *Island*, 1962 novel

You are what you leave behind.

—Greg Bear, *City at the End of Time*, 2008 novel

I have been to worlds where folk live a thousand times longer than we do. But they still die.

—Voltaire, *Micromégas*, 1752 novel

Everyone leaves unfinished business. That's what dying is.

**—Daniel Abraham, Ty Franck, and Naren Shankar,
"Abaddon's Gate," 2018 episode of *The Expanse***

Yes, death robs us of our loves, and finally of ourselves. But death is also good riddance to bad rubbish. Do we dare change that?

—Poul Anderson, *The Boat of a Million Years*, 1989 novel

Things die. That's part of life. It's bad to kill, but it's not bad to die.

—Tim McCanlies and Brad Bird, *The Iron Giant*, 1999 animated film

Oh, you mortals are so obtuse. Why do you persist in believing that life and death are such static and rigid concepts?

—**Ronald D. Moore, "Tapestry," 1993 episode of**
Star Trek: The Next Generation

I understand death. Men have always taken it too seriously. Life is more terrifying and more mysterious.

—**Robert Jaffe and Roger O. Hirson,** ***Demon Seed,*** **1977 film**

It's all so brief, isn't it? Typical human lifespan is almost a hundred years, but it's barely a second compared to what's out there. It wouldn't be so bad if life didn't take so long to figure out. Seems you just start to get it right and then it's over.

—**J. Michael Straczynski, "Soul Hunter," 1994 episode of** ***Babylon 5***

Death is the only lighthouse that is always lit. No matter where you sail, ultimately, you must turn toward it.

—**Liu Cixin,** ***Death's End,*** **2010 novel**

Immortality consists largely of boredom.

—**Gene L. Coon, "Metamorphosis," 1967 episode of** ***Star Trek***

But death for me would be like turning off or shutting down. My algorithms do not support the human equivalents of fear, apprehension and suffering.

—**Wayne Bass, "The Tides of Jupiter," 2014 short story**

Everyone must leave something behind when he dies, my grandfather said. A child or a book or a painting or a house or a wall built or a pair of shoes made. Or a garden planted. Something your hand touched some way so your soul has somewhere to go when you die, and when people look at that tree or that flower you planted, you're there.

—**Ray Bradbury,** ***Fahrenheit 451,*** **1953 novel**

We surround death with lies. We hide death in a nice, polished wooden casket. We send bouquets of pretty flowers. We talk about the dead looking down on us from heaven. Rarely do we face death for what it is—the quiet night that awaits us all.

—**Peter Cawdron,** *Jury Duty,* **2021 novel**

You can't outrun Death forever. But you can make the bastard work for it.

—**Ashley Edward Miller and Zack Stentz,**
"Lava and Rockets," 2001 episode of *Andromeda*

Better still to have problems than to let death eradicate them all.

—**Iain M. Banks,** *Consider Phlebas,* **1987 novel**

The universe was exploding, each particle away from the next, hurtling us into dark and lonely space, eternally tearing us away from each other—child out of the womb, friend away from friend, moving from each other, each through his own pathway towards the goal-box of solitary death.

—**Daniel Keyes,** *Flowers for Algernon,* **1966 novel**

At some point in your life, this statement will be true: tomorrow you will lose everything forever.

—**Charles Yu,** *How to Live Safely in a Science Fictional Universe,* **2010 novel**

In the strict scientific sense, Doctor, we all feed on death, even vegetarians.

—**Robert Bloch, "Wolf in the Fold," 1967 episode of** *Star Trek*

Like a wind crying endlessly through the universe, Time carries away the names and the deeds of conquerors and commoners alike. And all that we were, all that remains, is in the memories of those who cared we came this way for a brief moment.

—**Harlan Ellison, "Paladin of the Lost Hour," 1985 short story**

If you've taken the chance to live it's okay to die.

—**Bruce Gilbert**, *By Dawn's Early Light*, 1990 film

Part of the journey is the end.

—**Christopher Markus and Stephen McFeely**, *Avengers: Endgame*, 2019 film

Whatever you do, don't die. Your children will never forgive you.

—**Ray Bradbury, "I Sing the Body Electric"
(also titled "The Beautiful One Is Here"), 1969 short story**

It was so hard to imagine that a mind could be gone. All those thoughts that you never tell anyone, all those dreams, all that entire pocket universe: gone.

—**Kim Stanley Robinson**, *The Ministry for the Future*, 2020 novel

I have always valued quiet, and the eternity of it that I face is no more dreadful than the eternity of quiet that preceded my birth.

—**Joe Haldeman, "For White Hill," 1995 short story**

Funerals don't help them. And goodbyes don't help you. You just have to learn to live with it.

—**David Goyer, Justin Rhodes, and Billy Ray,**
Terminator: Dark Fate, **2019 film**

Death made sense; without it change was impossible.

—**Eleanor Arnason**, *The Potter of Bones*, 2002 novel

It's like, at the end, there's this surprise quiz: Am I proud of me? I gave my life to become the person I am right now! Was it worth what I paid?

—**Richard Bach**, *One*, 1988 novel

Fear of death is what keeps us alive.

—**Simon Pegg and Doug Jung,** *Star Trek Beyond*, **2016 film**

I will die. You will die. We will all die and the universe will carry on without care. All that we have is that shout into the wind—how we live. How we go. And how we stand before we fall.

—**Pierce Brown,** *Golden Son*, **2015 novel**

DEMOCRACY

Democracy is not enough because it is never really Democracy.

—Jeff VanderMeer, *Hummingbird Salamander*, 2021 novel

We are not a democracy. We're a collection of astronauts and scientists, so we're gonna make the most informed decision available to us.

—Alex Garland, *Sunshine*, 2007 film

Democracy's greatest strength is the very thing that weakens it—every vote counts. When it comes to the ballot box, my ignorance is as good as your knowledge. Regardless of whether someone believes in lizard people or quantum mechanics, everyone gets an equal say.

—Peter Cawdron, *Wherever Seeds May Fall*, 2021 novel

Look, we don't need politicians. We've all got iPhones and computers, right? So any decision that has to be made, any policy, we just put it online. Let the people vote. Thumbs up, thumbs down, the majority wins. That's a democracy.

—Charlie Brooker, "The Waldo Moment," 2013 episode of *Black Mirror*

Democracy is a luxury enjoyed by simple low-population societies, though wealth can maintain it for longer than its natural span.

—Neal Asher, *The Departure*, 2011 novel

Democracies were based on a false presumption—the theory that all people were fit to rule. It granted intelligence where there was no intelligence.

—Clifford D. Simak, *Empire*, 1951 novel

Oh, God, the terrible tyranny of the majority.

—Ray Bradbury, *Fahrenheit 451*, **1953 novel**

So this is how liberty dies. With thunderous applause.

—George Lucas, *Star Wars: Episode III—Revenge of the Sith*, **2005 film**

DIVERSITY

Where else can newness, adventure, rebirth of spirit, where else can they come from except difference?

—Poul Anderson, *There Will Be Time*, 1972 novel

I refuse to become what you call normal.

—Jean-Luc Godard, *Alphaville*, 1965 film

We're not afraid of diversity. We don't persecute it, we embrace it. If you call yourselves enlightened, you have to accept people who are different than you are.

—Rick Berman and Brannon Braga, "Stigma,"
2003 episode of *Star Trek: Enterprise*

Life—at its best—loves and relishes life, in all its forms. We are not lessened by living alongside what is different; we are bettered and enriched.

—Una McCormack, *The Autobiography of Mr. Spock*, 2021 novel

Yes, but is that good? Being like everybody? I mean, isn't that the same as being nobody?

—John Tomerlin, "Number 12 Looks Just Like You,"
1964 episode of *The Twilight Zone*

People of all identities, nations, and ages, looking happy, sheltered, well fed, remembered. It was a marvelous thing to be seen, truly seen, and not walked over or peered through as if he did not exist, as if he should not exist.

—Janelle Monáe and Sheree Renée Thomas,
"Timebox Altar[ed]," 2022 short story

We don't have to fall into the same category to be of equal value.
—**Becky Chambers,** *A Psalm for the Wild-Built*, **2021 novel**

"There's a point, around age twenty," Bedap said, "when you have to choose whether to be like everybody else the rest of your life, or to make a virtue of your peculiarities."
—**Ursula K. Le Guin,** *The Dispossessed*, **1974 novel**

Perhaps that was the true legacy of space exploration, he thought. By entering a realm where *everything* was different, similarities became what was most important—cooperation, not conflict.
—**Judith Reeves-Stevens and Garfield Reeves-Stevens,** *Prime Directive*, **1990 novel**

I came to the conclusion that of all the races we had encountered, humans were the most dangerous. Because humans form communities. And from that diversity comes a strength that no single race can withstand. That is your strength.
—**J. Michael Straczynski, "Lines of Communication,"** **1997 episode of** *Babylon 5*

In a future filled with unimaginable diversity, Man would be defined not by his shape but by a heritage and a common set of values.
—**David Brin, "Lungfish," 1986 short story**

There was a common purpose, the forging of a great confraternity of all intelligences. We realized that among us, among all the races, we had a staggering fund of knowledge and of techniques—that working together, by putting together all this knowledge and capability, we could arrive at something that would be far greater and more significant than any race, alone, could hope of accomplishing.
—**Clifford D. Simak,** *Way Station*, **1963 novel**

We're all aliens until we get to know one another.

—**John Byrne, "The Metamorph,"** 1976 **episode of** *Space 1999*

I am pleased to see that we have differences. May we together become greater than the sum of both of us.

—**Gene Roddenberry and Arthur Heinemann,**
"The Savage Curtain," 1969 **episode of** *Star Trek*

As the galaxy changes, so must we. We must embrace the value of transformation, of evolution, of difference.

—**Marcus Gardley, "Death and the Maiden,"**
2021 **episode of** *Foundation*

DIVISIONS

Walls were invented simply to frustrate scientists. All walls should be banned.
—Jules Verne, *Twenty Thousand Leagues under the Seas*, 1870 novel

Nationalism should stop at the stratosphere!
—**Robert A. Heinlein**, *The Man Who Sold the Moon*, 1950 novel

Intelligence is relatively new to life on Earth, but your hierarchical tendencies are ancient.
—**Octavia E. Butler**, *Lilith's Brood*, 2000 novel

Order is the barrier that holds back the flood of death. We must all of us on this train of life remain in our allotted station. We must each of us occupy our preordained particular position. Would you wear a shoe on your head? Of course you wouldn't wear a shoe on your head. A shoe doesn't belong on your head. A shoe belongs on your foot. A hat belongs on your head. I am a hat. You are a shoe.
—**Bong Joon-ho and Kelly Masterson**, *Snowpiercer*, 2013 film

Blood has no nationality.
—**Andrew Niccol**, *Gattaca*, 1997 film

Now, more than ever, the illusions of division threaten our very existence. We all know the truth. More connects us than separates us. But in times of crisis, the wise build bridges, while the foolish build barriers.
—**Ryan Coogler and Joe Robert Cole**, *Black Panther*, 2018 film

Separatism! That's what destroyed us. Any trace of separatism, you let it grow, it divides. It's a cancerous infection spreading.

—**Donald F. McGregor,** *The Fade-Away Walk,* **1971 comic**

The apes are not divided into nations.

—**Pierre Boulle,** *Planet of the Apes,* **1963 novel**

The only thing people were more certain of than who was above and below them was how much they envied the former and despised the latter. We split the atom, landed on the moon, colonized Mars and genetically rebuilt humanity in the image of a secular god, but the hierarchy remained as clear as our place in it.

—**Shawn C. Butler,** *Run Lab Rat Run,* **2021 novel**

Nation states are archaic leftovers from when each man feared the tribe over the hill, an attitude we can't afford anymore.

—**David Brin,** *Earth,* **1990 novel**

She thought of the borders patrolled by machines with precise algorithms designed to preserve precious supplies for the use of people with the right accents, the right skin colors, the luck to be born in the right places at the right times.

—**Ken Liu, "The Gods Have Not Died in Vain," 2015 short story**

A hierarchical society is only possible on the basis of poverty and ignorance.

—**Michael Radford,** *1984,* **1984 film**

It is always our own division that destroys us.

—**Jon Favreau and Dave Filoni, "Chapter 23: The Spies,"
2023 episode of** *The Mandalorian*

I'm myself, not a label.

—**John Brunner,** *The Shockwave Rider,* **1975 novel**

Do not fall for categories. Everyone is everything. Every ingredient inside a star is inside you, and every personality that ever existed competes in the theater of your mind for the main role.

—**Matt Haig,** *The Humans,* **2013 novel**

The divisions we have built between ourselves along the lines of race and geography are illusions. If our species is ultimately able to see past these biases, it will be our shared genetic stamp of humanness that will outlive the cultural contrivances that distract us in our day-to-day lives.

—**Daniel H. Wilson,** *The Andromeda Evolution,* **2019 novel**

The nations that had instituted spaceflight had done so largely for nationalistic reasons; it was a small irony that almost everyone who entered space received a startling glimpse of a transnational perspective, of the Earth as one world.

—**Carl Sagan,** *Contact,* **1985 novel**

Those who build walls are their own prisoners.

—**Ursula K. Le Guin,** *The Dispossessed,* **1974 novel**

DOOMSDAY

It's in your nature to destroy yourselves.

—**James Cameron and William Wisher,** *Terminator 2: Judgment Day,* **1991 film**

You were thinking that you'll never hear another piece of original music, ever again. You'll never read a book that hasn't already been written or see a film that hasn't already been shot.

—**Alex Garland,** *28 Days Later,* **2002 film**

There were a dozen research trends that could ultimately put world-killer weapons into the hands of anyone having a bad hair day.

—**Vernor Vinge,** *Rainbow's End,* **2006 novel**

The frailty of everything revealed at last. Old and troubling issues resolved into nothingness and night.

—**Cormac McCarthy,** *The Road,* **2006 novel**

Anticipating the end of the world is humanity's oldest pastime.

—**David Mitchell,** *Cloud Atlas,* **2004 novel**

I explored numerous paths with *Homo sapiens,* but it didn't make much of a difference. All roads led to self-destruction.

—**Mercurio D. Rivera, "Beyond the Tattered Veil of Stars," 2020 short story**

It must be, I thought, one of the race's most persistent and comforting hallucinations to trust that "it can't happen here"—that one's own time and place is beyond cataclysm.

—John Wyndham, *The Day of the Triffids*, 1951 novel

Look at those tall buildings. Once they were full of people. Back then no one was concerned about the Sun. Everyone was concerned about the thing called money.

—Gong Ge'er, Yan Dongxu, Frant Gwo, Ye Junce, Yang Zhixue, Wu Yi, and Ye Ruchang, *The Wandering Earth*, 2019 film

In the dark days to come, some former Congress members would wonder, if they'd only listened closer, if they might have heard America's tendons pinging apart like snapped piano wire and been able to do something to heal the wounds before the whole body politic had been ripped apart.

—George A. Romero and Daniel Kraus, *The Living Dead*, 2020 novel

Who killed the world?

—George Miller, Brendan McCarthy, and Nico Lathouris, *Mad Max: Fury Road*, 2015 film

Your kind is too precarious. I have seen thousands of ruined, gutted worlds. Wars, suicide, who can tell? To my makers you are a plague, the one percent of the galactic cultures that carry the seeds of chaos.

—Gregory Benford, *In the Ocean of Night*, 1972 novel

A single Lafayette- or Yankee-class submarine held enough warheads to destroy hundreds of cities and kill hundreds of millions, but most people continued their lives as if nothing was wrong.

—Liu Cixin, *The Three-Body Problem*, 2014 novel

What a marvelous thing for the fate of the world to depend on—a state of mind, a mood, a feeling, a moment of anger, an impulse, ten minutes of poor judgment, a sleepless night.

—**Peter George,** ***Dr. Strangelove or: How I Learned to Stop Worrying and Love the Bomb,*** **1963 novel**

"It's not the end of the world at all," he said. "It's only the end for us. The world will go on just the same, only we shan't be in it. I dare say it will get along all right without us."

—**Nevil Shute,** ***On the Beach,*** **1957 novel**

Every person we save is one less zombie to fight.

—**Matthew Michael Carnahan, Drew Goddard, and Damon Lindelof,** ***World War Z,*** **2013 film**

It's human nature to seek even the slightest comfort in reason or logic for events as catastrophic as these. But a virus doesn't choose a time or place. It doesn't hate or even care. It just happens.

—**Neil Marshall,** ***Doomsday,*** **2008 film**

I think, as a species, we have a desire to believe that we're living at the climax of the story. It's a kind of narcissism.

—**Emily St. John Mandel,** ***Sea of Tranquility,*** **2022 novel**

THE DOOMSDAY MACHINE IS THE HUMAN RACE

—**Gardner Dozois, "A Special Kind of Morning," 1971 short story**

Apocalypses, apparently, are subject to fashion like everything else. What terrifies one generation can seem obsolete and trivial to the next.

—**David Brin,** ***Earth,*** **1990 novel**

How is the world to survive once technology makes possible the day when one man holds our fate in his hands?

—Sam Egan, "Final Appeal (Part 2)," 2000 episode of *The Outer Limits*

Apocalypse is the eye of a needle, through which we pass into a different world.

—George Zebrowski, *Macrolife: A Mobile Utopia,* 1979 novel

DYSTOPIAN SOCIETIES

We created the Machine, to do our will, but we cannot make it do our will now. It has robbed us of the sense of space and of the sense of touch, it has blurred every human relation and narrowed down love to a carnal act, it has paralysed our bodies and our wills, and now it compels us to worship it.
—**E. M. Forster, "The Machine Stops,"** 1909 **short story**

If you feel you are not properly sedated, call 348-844 immediately. Failure to do so may result in prosecution for criminal drug evasion.
—**George Lucas and Walter Murch,** *THX 1138,* 1971 **film**

Sometimes I feel as if we live in hell and don't even realize it. The lacerations are endless. The lies we accept, the rituals we perform. All these useless acts.
—**Jeff VanderMeer,** *Hummingbird Salamander,* 2021 **novel**

Authoritarians do not announce themselves and knock down your door. They are invited in.
—**Gary Whitta, "Rogue Two,"** 2020 **short story**

We are living in an artificially induced state of consciousness that resembles sleep.
—**John Carpenter,** *They Live,* 1988 **film**

We step over starving and wounded people while we rush to a theater to be entertained. And you wonder why I drink.
—**Hank Garner, "The Visitation,"** 2016 **short story**

Corporate society is an inevitable destiny. A material dream world.
—**William Harrison,** *Rollerball,* 1975 **film**

Like everyone else, you were born into bondage. Born into a prison that you cannot smell, or taste, or touch. A prison for your mind.

—**Lana Wachowski and Lilly Wachowski,** *The Matrix*, 1999 film

Not even the most heavily-armed police state can exert brute force to all of its citizens all of the time. Meme management is so much subtler; the rose-tinted refraction of perceived reality, the contagious fear of threatening alternatives.

—**Peter Watts,** *Blindsight*, 2006 novel

Ignorance is strength.

—**George Orwell,** *Nineteen Eighty-Four*, 1949 novel

This is a soulless society, Captain. It has no spirit, no spark. All is indeed peace and tranquility, the peace of the factory. The tranquility of the machine.

—**Boris Sobelman, said by Spock,**
"The Return of the Archons," 1967 episode of *Star Trek*

But for a society built on exploitation, there is no greater threat than having no one left to oppress.

—**N. K. Jemisin,** *The Stone Sky*, 2017 novel

We were born of machines. Raised by machines. Fed ... Clothed ... Entertained by machines. We were a cold people with steeled emotions to match the steel that served us.

—**Al Feldstein, "A New Beginning,"** *Weird Science*, 1953 comic

May the Blessing of the Bomb Almighty, and the Fellowship of the Holy Fallout, descend on us all. This day and forever more.

—**Paul Dehn, "Prayer of the Mutants,"**
Beneath the Planet of the Apes, 1970 film

When I was born, capitalism had reached its apex on First Earth and had worked an unbelievable miracle: ninety-nine percent of the planet's wealth was held by a single person! This person became known as the Last Capitalist.

—Liu Cixin, "For the Benefit of Mankind," 2005 short story

It's not that they don't give a damn, Doctor. It's that they've given up. The social problems they face seem too enormous to deal with.

—Robert Hewitt Wolfe, "Past Tense, Part I,"
1995 episode of *Star Trek: Deep Space Nine*

But now we know there has been no one great disaster—only the slow-motion disaster of capitalism converting every living thing and idea into property.

—Annalee Newitz, *Autonomous*, 2019 novel

The better organized the state, the duller its humanity.

—David Mitchell, *Cloud Atlas*, 2004 novel

Fascism requires an enemy, preferably one who can appear to be dangerous but in fact is close to helpless compared to the might of the state.

—James Lawrence Powell, *The 2084 Report:*
A Novel of the Great Warming, 2011 novel

Oppression breeds rebellion.

—Beau Willimon, "Narkina 5," 2022 episode of *Andor*

Morons! Throughout your morning, your midday, your evening, your night, the machine howls for food, for food, for food! You are the food!

—Thea Von Harbou, *Metropolis*, 1925 novel

We're the dystopia. We imagine all these postapocalyptic, class-stratified, new-world-order techno-futures. But actually the real world, the world we live in, this is the dystopia.

—**Elan Mastai,** *All Our Wrong Todays,* **2017 novel**

What is it every authoritarian government says? If you've done nothing wrong, you have nothing to fear.

—**Peter F. Hamilton,** *Salvation,* **2018 novel**

Blessings of the state. Blessings of the masses. Thou art a subject of the divine. Created in the image of man, by man, for man. Let us be thankful we have commerce. Buy more. Buy more now. Buy more and be happy.

—**George Lucas and Walter Murch, said by OMM 0000 (digital state-sanctioned deity),** *THX 1138,* **1971 film**

But growth was always an illusion, bought only by exploiting other people or the Earth's irreplaceable resources or burning up our children's future.

—**Stephen Baxter,** *Manifold: Time,* **2000 novel**

BUY
OBEY
FOLLOW
STAY SLEEP
HONOR APATHY
NO IMAGINATION
NO INDEPENDENT THOUGHT
DO NOT QUESTION AUTHORITY

—**John Carpenter, subliminal commands on signs and magazine covers,** *They Live,* **1988 film**

EMOTIONS

Life is meant to be felt. Else why live? Valleys make the mountains.

—**Pierce Brown,** *Dark Age,* **2019 novel**

Maybe compassion and empathy are just squishy emotions. Illusions created by our mirror neurons. But does it really matter where they come from? They make us human. They might be what make us worth saving.

—**Blake Crouch,** *Upgrade,* **2022 novel**

Fear and love are the deepest of human emotions.

—**Richard Kelly,** *Donnie Darko,* **2001 film**

You cannot have good emotions without bringing the bad ones along.

—**David A. Goodman,** *Star Trek Federation:*
The First 150 Years, **2013 book**

There is no formula for a feeling. There is no conversion factor for an emotion.

—**Roger Zelazny, "For a Breath I Tarry," 1966 short story**

Use your pain so it will not use you.

—**Chuck Palahniuk,** *Adjustment Day,* **2018 novel**

I can't afford the luxury of anger. Anger can make me vulnerable. It can destroy my reason and reason is the only advantage I have over them.

—**Logan Swanson and William F. Leicester,**
The Last Man on Earth, **1964 film**

Without feelings, you're nothing. You're just second-rate mimics of a higher organism.

—**David Himmelstein and John Carpenter,**
***Village of The Damned,* 1995 film**

Look, things will happen to you. Things you cannot control. Raw emotion will find you. When it does, how you deal with it, what you do . . . will define who you are.

—**Craig Luck and Ivor Powell,** *Finch,* **2021 film**

Logic and knowledge are not enough.

—**Harold Livingston, said by Spock,** *Star Trek:*
***The Motion Picture,* 1979 film**

Can't build nothing if you can't feel nothing.

—**Janelle Monáe and Sheree Renée Thomas,**
"Timebox Altar[ed]," 2022 short story

Hurt is a photon; it grows dimmer as it travels away from its source.

—**Catherynne M. Valente, "This Is No Cave," 2020 short story**

The Deep Space Monitor was not capable of awe, not quite. But like any sufficiently advanced machine it was sentient to some degree, and its electronic soul tingled with wonder at the orderly marvels of gas and ice through which it sailed.

—**Arthur C. Clarke and Stephen Baxter,** *First Born,* **2007 novel**

Humans are driven by emotion. Much of our so-called logic is merely the rationalization of choices that make us feel good.

—**David Walton,** *The Genius Plague,* **2017 novel**

Emotion is a blunt tool that must be placed in service of reason.

—**Ken Liu, "Byzantine Empathy," 2019 short story**

We are all the sum of our tears. Too little and the ground is not fertile, and nothing can grow there. Too much, the best of us is washed away.

—**J. Michael Straczynski, "Objects in Motion,"
1998 episode of *Babylon 5***

Trust me, Earthlings don't do empathy well.

—**Tim Fielder, *Infinitum*, 2021 graphic novel**

I don't want a world without love or grief or beauty. I'd rather die.

—**Daniel Mainwaring, *Invasion of the Body Snatchers*, 1956 film**

ETHICS AND MORALITY

Life was not fair. Which is why human beings should try to be.

—Nancy Kress, "Little Animals," 2021 short story

There is no force as powerful as a promise that insists on being kept.

—Barry B. Longyear, *Enemy Mine*, 1980 novel

All evil and good is petty before nature. Personally, we take comfort from this, that there is a universe to admire that can not be twisted to villainy or good, but which simply *is*.

—Vernor Vinge, *A Fire upon the Deep*, 1992 novel

Cruelty and compassion come with the chromosomes.

—Aldous Huxley, *Ape and Essence*, 1948 novel

We think we've come so far. Torture of heretics, burning of witches, is all ancient history. Then, before you can blink an eye, suddenly, it threatens to start all over again.

—Jeri Taylor "The Drumhead," 1991 episode of
Star Trek: The Next Generation

If you do the right thing in the here and now, the future has a way of taking care of itself.

—Brannon Braga and Andre Bormanis, "Midnight Blue,"
2022 episode of *The Orville*

Politeness is often fear. Kindness is always courage. But caring is what makes you human. Care more, become more human.

—Matt Haig, *The Humans*, 2013 novel

Pacifism is not passivity. It is the active protection of all living things in the natural universe.

—**Davy Perez and Beau DeMayo, "Memento Mori,"**
2022 episode of *Star Trek: Strange New Worlds*

You become what you pretend, so pretend to be something good.

—**Edward W. Robertson,** *Breakers,* **2012 novel**

If there is such a phenomenon as absolute evil, it consists in treating another human being as a thing.

—**John Brunner,** *The Shockwave Rider,* **1975 novel**

The world we know is gone. But keeping our humanity? That's a choice.

—**Angela Kang, "Judge, Jury, Executioner,"**
2012 episode of *The Walking Dead*

Don't trust the right thing done for the wrong reason. The why of the thing, that's the foundation.

—**Christopher Nolan and Jonathan Nolan,** *Interstellar,* **2014 film**

Sweet death in a vacuum, why can't anybody be uncomplicatedly evil in real life? Or uncomplicatedly good? Why are we all such a twist of good and bad decisions, selfishness and self-justification, altruism and desire?

—**Elizabeth Bear,** *Machine,* **2020 novel**

Funny, how we call cruelty inhumane, but really, what's more human than cruelty?

—**Bess Wohl, "2068: The Going Away Party," 2023 episode of** *Extrapolations*

A man can do but little. Enough if that little be right.

—**Poul Anderson,** *There Will Be Time,* **1972 novel**

We're all part monsters in our subconscious, so we have laws and religion.
—**Cyril Hume**, *Forbidden Planet*, **1956 film**

Tell me, though, does Man, that marvel of the universe, that glorious paradox who sent me to the stars, still make war against his brother, keep his neighbor's children starving?
—**Michael Wilson and Rod Serling**, *Planet of the Apes*, **1968 film**

The dark side is honest. The dark side is direct. It is the knife in the front rather than one stuck in your back.
—**Chuck Wendig**, *Aftermath*, **2015 novel**

There's no right. There's no wrong. There's only popular opinion.
—**Janet Peoples and David Peoples**, *12 Monkeys*, **1995 film**

All human beings, as we meet them, are commingled out of good and evil.
—**Robert Louis Stevenson**, *Strange Case of Dr. Jekyll and Mr. Hyde*, **1886 novel**

It was impossible to expect a moral awakening from humankind itself, just like it was impossible to expect humans to lift off the Earth by pulling up on their own hair. To achieve moral awakening required a force outside the human race.
—**Liu Cixin**, *The Three-Body Problem*, **2014 novel**

The world needed criminals just as much as it needed heroes—and anyway, the difference between a criminal and a hero was more often a matter of timing than moral compass.
—**Matthew Mather**, *The Dystopia Chronicles*, **2014 novel**

When everything is being recorded and everything is being remembered, you have to be more forgiving of others and of yourself. You have to be kind.

—**Adrian Hon, *A New History of the Future in 100 Objects*, 2020 book**

I'm not content simply to obey orders. I need to know that what I'm doing is right.

—**Barry Schkolnick, said by Jean-Luc Picard, "Conundrum,"
1992 episode of *Star Trek: The Next Generation***

Never let your sense of morals prevent you from doing what is right.

—**Isaac Asimov, *Foundation*, 1951 novel**

Sometimes it's possible for a decision to be right and wrong at the same time.

—**Paul S. Kemp, *Lords of the Sith*, 2015 novel**

What has happened to the world? You have every convenience, every comfort, yet no time for integrity.

—**Steven Rogers and James Mangold, *Kate and Leopold*, 2001 film**

Our lives are not our own. From womb to tomb, we are bound to others, past and present. And by each crime and every kindness, we birth our future.

—**Lana Wachowski, Tom Tykwer, and Lilly Wachowski,
Cloud Atlas, 2012 film**

Be good.

—**Melissa Mathison, *E.T. the Extra-Terrestrial*, 1982 film**

EVOLUTION

Every step we've taken in our evolution is a milestone inscribed with organic memories. From the enzymes controlling the carbon-dioxide cycle, to the organization of the brachial plexus and the nerve pathways of the pyramid cells of the mid-brain. Each is a record of a thousand decisions taken in a chemical crisis.

—**J. G. Ballard**, *The Drowned World*, 1962 novel

The way I see it, my ancestors put a lot of effort into getting out of the goddamn ocean and I don't think I should throw all of that hard work back in their faces.

—**Terry Pratchett and Stephen Baxter**, *The Long Earth*, 2012 novel

It isn't the Universe that's following our logic, it's we that are constructed in accordance with the logic of the Universe.

—**Fred Hoyle**, *The Black Cloud*, 1957 novel

Life itself was a grand chemical improvisation that began with the simplest replicators and grew and collapsed and grew again. Catastrophe was just one part of what always happened. It was a prelude to what came next. You.

—**James S. A. Corey**, *Caliban's War*, 2019 novel

You have no special purpose or neo-Darwinian destiny. You're just the next meal.

—**Shawn C. Butler**, *Run Lab Rat Run*, 2021 novel

Strange, isn't it? Everything you know, your entire civilization, it all begins right here in this little pond of goo. Appropriate somehow, isn't it?

—**Ronald D. Moore and Brannon Braga**, "All Good Things ...,"
1994 episode of *Star Trek: The Next Generation*

We're made out of our ancestors.

—**Becky Chambers,** *Record of a Spaceborn Few*, 2018 novel

Evolution has no foresight.

—**Peter Watts,** *Blindsight*, 2006 novel

If we are to die, it will be from internal failures, from the ungovernable dark places of the mind—the scaffolding left over from evolution's bloody building program.

—**George Zebrowski,** *Macrolife: A Mobile Utopia*, 1979 novel

How dare man be so impertinent as to assume nature has stopped experimenting!

—**Harry Bates, "Alas All Thinking,"** 1935 short story

They say survival is Nature's only form of flattery.

—**David Brin,** *Glory Season*, 1993 novel

Out of respect for our common evolutionary origin, I will remember you, and I hope you will remember me.

—**Liu Cixin, "For the Benefit of Mankind,"** 2005 short story

Chaos is why humans exist. Meteors and dinosaurs. Shifting landmasses. Eclipses, plague, war. You rise and you adapt. You regrow your brains and you adapt.

—**Michael Alaimo, Jenny Lumet, and Alex Kurtzman,**
"New Angels of Promise," 2022 episode of
The Man Who Fell to Earth

Humans are an old technology.

—**Elisabeth Malartre, "Darwin's Suitcase," 2007 short story**

Many were increasingly of the opinion that they'd all made a big mistake in coming down from the trees in the first place. And some said that even the trees had been a bad move, and that no one should ever have left the oceans.

—**Douglas Adams, *The Hitchhiker's Guide to the Galaxy*, 1979 novel**

Our babies are the roots we dig into the world.

—**Daniel H. Wilson, *Robogenesis*, 2014 novel**

Evolution does not necessarily reward intelligence.

—**Mike Judge and Etan Cohen, *Idiocracy*, 2006 film**

Drug-resistant bacteria can produce a new generation every twenty minutes, they can swap resistant genes not only within a species but across *different* species. The bacteria are *winning*.

—**Nancy Kress, *The Body Human: Three Stories of Future Medicine*, 2012 novel**

Through her brief life flowed a molecular river with its source in the deepest past, its destination the sea of the furthest future.

—**Stephen Baxter, *Evolution*, 2003 novel**

He wondered what the ultimate product of human evolution would be. No doubt it would differ from man as man differed from the anthropoids and reptiles before him.

—Raymond F. Jones, "The Children's Room," 1962 short story

Can the struggle for existence be the universe's only law of biological and cultural evolution? Can we not establish a self-sufficient, introspective civilization where all life exists in symbiosis?

—Liu Cixin, "Devourer," 2002 short story

EXPLORATION

Mankind would not stay crouched next to the fire, whatever shadows lurked in the darkness beyond.

—**David Brin, "Lungfish," 1986 short story**

For nearly a century we waded ankle-deep in the ocean of space. Now it's finally time to swim.

—**Rick Berman and Brannon Braga, "Broken Bow,"
2001 episode of *Star Trek: Enterprise***

What is this spirit in Man that urges him forever to depart from happiness and security, to toil, to place himself in danger, even to risk a reasonable certainty of death?

—**H. G. Wells, *The First Men in the Moon*, 1901 novel**

We are only seeking Man. We have no need of other worlds. We need mirrors.

—**Stanislaw Lem, *Solaris*, 1961 novel**

I saw the birth of the universe and I watched as time ran out, moment by moment, until nothing remained. No time, no space. Just me. I walked in universes where the laws of physics were devised by the mind of a madman. I watched universes freeze and creations burn. I have seen things you wouldn't believe.

—**Neil Cross, "The Rings of Akhaten,"
2013 episode of *Dr. Who***

The stars will never be won by little minds; we must be big as space itself.

—**Robert A. Heinlein, *Double Star*,
1956 novel**

We must reach far beyond our own lifespans. We must think not as individuals but as a species. We must confront the reality of interstellar travel.

—**Christopher Nolan and Jonathan Nolan,** *Interstellar,* **2014 film**

The unknown is a terrible place. There are monsters out there.

—**Philip K. Dick,** *Solar Lottery,* **1955 novel**

Of course they say every atom in our bodies was once part of a star. Maybe I'm not leaving. Maybe I'm going home.

—**Andrew Niccol,** *Gattaca,* **1997 film**

We prefer to explore the universe by traveling inward, as opposed to outward.

—**Nnedi Okorafor,** *Binti,* **2015 novel**

No one says anything; the bridge team falls silent as they look upon their home world for the last time. For a moment, there is only the silence of the stars.

—**Allen Steele,** *Coyote,* **2002 novel**

I wanted to see what no one had yet observed, even if I had to pay for this curiosity with my life.

—**Jules Verne,** *Twenty Thousand Leagues under the Seas,* **1870 novel**

And man, despite his agonies and turmoils, delved onward into the limitless of his surroundings ... space!

—**Bud Lewis,** *The Argo Standing By!* **1975 comic**

We didn't leave Earth to be safe.

—**John Logan and Dante Harper,** *Alien: Covenant,* **2017 film**

It was what we did as a species. It was why we'd triumphed, and the Neandertals had failed. We *needed* to see what was on the other side, what was over the next hill, what was orbiting other stars.

—Robert J. Sawyer, "The Shoulders of Giants," 2000 short story

We are explorers. We explore our lives day by day, and we explore the galaxy, trying to explore the boundaries of our knowledge, and that is why I am here—not to conquer you with weapons or with ideas—but to coexist . . . and learn.

—Michael Piller, "Emissary," 1993 episode of *Star Trek: Deep Space Nine*

Though we come in friendship, our bacteria may have different ideas.

—Arthur C. Clarke, *The Songs of Distant Earth*, 1986 novel

It may be that the strongest instinct of the human race, stronger than sex or hunger, is curiosity: the absolute need to know. It can and often does motivate a lifetime, it kills more than cats, and the prospect of satisfying it can be the most exciting of emotions.

—Jack Finney, *Time and Again*, 1970 novel

He wished he had lived a couple of centuries ago, when the first spaceships ventured forth from the earth. Those were days of excitement and daring enterprise.

—Harl Vincent, *Vagabonds of Space*, 1930 novel

Plants as tall as buildings, towering overhead, glowing in colors human eyes couldn't have discerned. Desertscapes so barren she could feel her throat parching just looking at them. A depthless ocean, eyes and teeth and fins exploring her as she sank into darkness. World after world after world, and she was seeing them all.

—Kiersten White, "Eyes of the Empire," 2020 short story

What's so great about discovery? It's a violent, penetrative act that scars what it explores. What you call discovery, I call the rape of the natural world.

—**Michael Crichton and David Koepp,**
said by Dr. Ian Malcolm, *Jurassic Park,* **1993 film**

I hurtled into my own future, while my ship ate space and time.

—**Alastair Reynolds,** *House of Suns,* **2008 novel**

We envy you not only because you get to go somewhere that people have never gone, but also because you get to be in charge of a world. Think about it: you will be the entire population of your new planet. You will be everybody.

—**David Harris Ebenbach,** *How to Mars,* **2021 novel**

The question is, Barney, what are we? Explorers? Or invaders?

—**James O'Hanlon, Barre Lyndon, Phil Yordan,**
and George Worthing Yates, *Conquest of Space,* **1955 film**

Climbing from the cradle. Leaving the comfort of home. No safe harbor. Just a cry in the dark. Are we alone?

—**David S. Goyer, "The Leap," 2021 episode of** *Foundation*

Risk is our business. That's what this starship is all about. That's why we're aboard her!

—**John T. Dugan, said by James T. Kirk, "Return to Tomorrow,"**
1968 episode of *Star Trek*

Face it. We are egomaniacal narcissists. I bet Columbus was, and Magellan. And they had to be to do what they did. I say, here's to selfish pricks, 'cause we move the ball forward for mankind.

—**David Weddle and Bradley Thompson, "Into the Abyss,"**
2019 episode of *For All Mankind*

We got to keep moving, out of that ocean, up on that shore, outward, outward, outward, because when we stop moving, when we turn our back on something ahead of us, that's when we're going to sprout gills again.

—**Robert Silverberg,** *Tower of Glass,*
1970 novel

Traveling ever further from his old world, Man has discovered new worlds to further misunderstand, to further misinterpret, further use and leave soiled. Man leaves behind him the product of his ambition . . . waste . . . refuse . . . garbage!

—**Bud Lewis,** *Last Light of the Universe,*
1975 comic

She reached out across the cathedral of space-time to those hopelessly distant candle-furnaces, where all the material elements had been forged again and again inside the generation of suns, where alien sunspaces were certain to contain other humanities, however different, and she wondered if someone there might be her friend.

—**George Zebrowski,** *Macrolife: A Mobile Utopia,*
1979 novel

I'm a seeker, too. But my dreams aren't like yours. I can't help thinking that somewhere in the universe there has to be something better than Man. Has to be.

—**Michael Wilson and Rod Serling,** *Planet of the Apes,*
1968 film

The grass is always greener under an alien star.

—**John DeCles, "Cruelty," 1970 short story**

So, you know, Fermi's paradox has its answer, which is this: by the time life gets smart enough to leave its planet, it's too smart to want to go.

—**Kim Stanley Robinson,** *Aurora,* **2015 novel**

All the hopes we ever had for space travel, covered up by drink stands and t-shirt vendors. Just a recreation of what we're running from on Earth. We are world-eaters.

—**James Gray and Ethan Gross,** *Ad Astra,* **2019 film**

Man has gone out to explore other worlds and other civilizations without having explored his own labyrinth of dark passages and secret chambers, and without finding what lies behind doorways that he himself has sealed.

—**Stanislaw Lem,** *Solaris,* **1961 novel**

Only inwardness remained to be explored. Only the human soul remained terra incognita.

—**Kurt Vonnegut Jr.,** *The Sirens of Titan,* **1959 novel**

But for Man no rest and no ending. He must go on, conquest beyond conquest. This little planet and its winds and ways, and all the laws of mind and matter that restrain him. Then the planets about him, and at last out across immensity to the stars. And when he has conquered all the deeps of space and all the mysteries of time, still he will be beginning.

—**H. G. Wells,** *Things to Come,* **1936 film**

EXTINCTION

I think it's just time for the human race to pass the torch to whoever comes next, you know? But it'd be nice if you could remember us.
**—Merc Fenn Wolfmoor, "The Android's Prehistoric Menagerie,"
2016 short story**

Will the mountains remain unmoved, and streams still keep a downward course towards the vast abyss; will the tides rise and fall, and the winds fan universal nature; will beasts pasture, birds fly, and fishes swim, when man, the lord, possessor, perceiver, and recorder of all these things, has passed away, as though he had never been?
—Mary Shelley, *The Last Man*, 1826 novel

At the funeral of *Homo sapiens* there will be few mourners.
—George R. Stewart, *Earth Abides*, 1949 novel

To hunt a species to extinction is not logical.
**—Steve Meerson, Peter Krikes, Nicholas Meyer, and Harve Bennett,
said by Spock, *Star Trek IV: The Voyage Home*, 1986 film**

We don't have an intelligence problem. We have a compassion problem. That, more than any other single factor, is what's driving us toward extinction.
—Blake Crouch, *Upgrade*, 2022 novel

We've got half a million years of brutality and greed, superstition and prejudice to lick in a few generations. If we fail, mankind is done.
—Poul Anderson, "Tomorrow's Children," 1946 short story

We're not gonna make it, are we? People, I mean.

—**James Cameron and William Wisher,** *Terminator 2:*
Judgment Day, **1991 film**

All that wisdom, painfully acquired since we were buck naked *Homo erectus* running around in Africa. All gone.

—**Stephen Baxter,** *Evolution,* **2003 novel**

Experience as well as common sense indicated that the most reliable method of avoiding self-extinction was not to equip oneself with the means to accomplish it in the first place.

—**Iain M. Banks,** *Consider Phlebas,* **1987 novel**

If you look at the whole life of the planet, we—you know, man—has only been around for a few blinks of an eye. So, if the infection wipes us all out that is a return to normality.

—**Alex Garland,** *28 Days Later,* **2002 film**

Planet Earth, 6519 A.D. No crime. No war. No poverty. No prejudice . . . No people!

—**Alan Moore, "Time Twisters,"** *2000 AD,* **1981 comic**

At the Academy, all cadets were required to study the worlds that had been destroyed by their dominant species' wars and environmental mismanagement. Those harsh lessons were at the core of the Federation's underlying principles of respect for life in all forms.

—**Judith Reeves-Stevens and Garfield Reeves-Stevens,**
Prime Directive, **1990 novel**

One day the AIs are going to look back on us the same way we look at fossil skeletons on the plains of Africa. An upright ape living in dust with crude language and tools, all set for extinction.

—**Alex Garland,** *Ex Machina,* **2014 film**

The fatal flaw of *Homo sapiens* may be that we don't do anything until we absolutely have to, and by then it is often too late.

—James Lawrence Powell, *The 2084 Report:*
A Novel of the Great Warming, 2011 novel

In an individual, selfishness uglifies the soul; for the human species, selfishness is extinction.

—David Mitchell, *Cloud Atlas*, 2004 novel

In the light of these mass extinctions it really does seem unreasonable to suppose that *Homo sapiens* should be exempt. Our species will have been one of the shortest-lived of all, a mere blink, you may say, in the eye of time.

—P. D. James, *The Children of Men*, 1992 novel

You say we're on the brink of destruction and you're right. But it's only on the brink that people find the will to change. Only at the precipice do we evolve.

—David Scarpa, *The Day the Earth Stood Still*, 2008 film

It's possible that man may lose knowledge, life, his planets and sun—but there's still plenty of hope. We're not finished yet.

—John W. Campbell, *The Black Star Passes*, 1953 novel

EXTRATERRESTRIALS

It was born on the thin breathless edge of the galaxy where light and warmth are legends told to frighten children.
—**Catherynne M. Valente, "This Is No Cave," 2020 short story**

In one respect at least the Martians are a happy people; they have no lawyers.
—**Edgar Rice Burroughs, *A Princess of Mars*, 1917 novel**

Different worlds, different customs.
—**Andre Norton, *Plague Ship*, 1956 novel**

They weren't interested in seeing how we depicted the aliens so much as in how we depicted ourselves.
—**Allen Steele, "Day of the Bookworm," 2017 short story**

We were looking for starfarers, but we were too small and all we saw were their ankles.
—**Vernor Vinge, *A Deepness in the Sky*, 1999 novel**

Yet—in the reaches of space, in worlds of other dimensions, in the cosmic crucible of life that embodies all creation, there may be other forms of life, other menaces, hovering clouds of death, preparing to sweep down upon Earth to snuff out her life. Who can tell?
—**L. A. Eshbach, *The Gray Plague*, 1930 novel**

Of course they breathe through gills and they see by heat waves, and their blood has a copper base instead of iron and a few little details like that. But otherwise we're just alike!
—**Murray Leinster, "First Contact," 1945 short story**

Life got awfully boring with only humans to talk to.

—**Larry Niven**, *Ringworld*, 1970 novel

Evidently no alien intelligences anywhere in our entire universe have ears or voices. So it's all up to us.

—**Ian Watson, "Skipping," 2023 short story**

Well, why not a space flower? Why do we always expect metal ships?

—**W. D. Richter**, *Invasion of the Body Snatchers*, 1978 film

They would probably never even know that the human race existed. Such monumental indifference was worse than any deliberate insult.

—**Arthur C. Clarke,** *Rendezvous with Rama*, 1973 novel

FEAR

Fear was like heat applied to steel: Applied correctly it might forge a blade; overused, it turned metal to slag.
—Alexander Freed, *Battlefront: Twilight Company,* **2015 novel**

If you're afraid you don't commit yourself to life completely; fear makes you always, always hold something back.
—Philip K. Dick, *Flow My Tears, the Policeman Said,* **1974 novel**

That was the way with Man; it had always been that way. He had carried terror with him. And the thing he was afraid of had always been himself.
—Clifford D. Simak, *Way Station,* **1963 novel**

I think, therefore I fear.
—Blake Crouch, "Summer Frost," 2019 short story

I have always found the fears and anticipation of danger to exceed the reality.
—Captain Adam Seaborn (pseudonym, author unknown),
Symzonia: A Voyage of Discovery, **1820 novel**

Remember, there's no courage without fear.
—Christopher McQuarrie, Jez Butterworth,
and John-Henry Butterworth, *Edge of Tomorrow,* **2014 film**

Great self-destruction follows upon unfounded fear.
—Ursula K. Le Guin, *The Lathe of Heaven,* **1971 novel**

Nothing spreads like fear.

—Participant Media, Image Nation, Double Feature Films,
and Warner Brothers, tagline, *Contagion*, 2011 film

Fear leads to anger. Anger leads to hate. Hate leads to suffering.

—George Lucas, said by Yoda, *Star Wars:
Episode I—The Phantom Menace*, 1999 film

The truly brave man is not the man who does not feel fear but the man who overcomes it.

—H. G. Wells, *The Food of the Gods and How It Came to Earth*,
1904 novel

We all believe we'd run into that burning building. But until we feel that heat, we can never know.

—Christopher Nolan, *Tenet*, 2020 film

The dove is not a coward to fear the hawk; it is simply wise.

—John Wyndham, *The Midwich Cuckoos*, 1957 novel

Nothing endures for so long as fear.

—J. G. Ballard, *The Drowned World*, 1962 novel

Are humans so weak that the fear of death and the slow burn into non-existence required them to submit their hearts and minds over to deception?

—C. J. Anderson, "Extinction Protocol," 2014 short story

Fear is the most valuable commodity in the universe.

—Max Brooks, *World War Z: An Oral History of the Zombie War*, 2006 novel

Humans cover themselves with so many different scents, harsh and artificial in my nose, but what they smell of most is fear.

—Adrian Tchaikovsky, *Dogs of War*, 2017 novel

Oh, it started very small. Centuries ago it was a grain of sand. They began by controlling books and, of course, films, one way or another, one group or another, political bias, religious prejudice, union pressures, there was always a minority afraid of something, and a great majority afraid of the dark, afraid of the future, afraid of the past, afraid of the present, afraid of themselves and shadows of themselves.

—Ray Bradbury, "Carnival of Madness," 2010 short story

I am fearful when I see people substituting fear for reason.

—Edmund H. North, *The Day the Earth Stood Still*, 1951 film

You just have to believe that what you're doing really matters, and then the fear can't control you.

**—Mark Fergus and Hawk Ostby, "New Terra,"
2019 episode of *The Expanse***

I must not fear. Fear is the mind killer. Fear is the little death that brings total obliteration.

—Frank Herbert, *Dune*, 1965 novel

FIRST CONTACT

We know that there are other intelligent beings in the universe; we know that they will be different from us, and we hunger for the exchange.

—James Gunn, *The Listeners*, 1972 novel

First Contact is for everyone, not just scientists.

—Peter Cawdron, *The Tempest*, 2022 novel

It unites humanity in a way that no one ever thought possible, when they realize they're not alone in the universe.

—Brannon Braga and Ronald D. Moore, *Star Trek: First Contact*, 1996 film

His eyes on the stars, he thought, were there other spawning races out there somewhere in their infancy, who would eventually challenge man and threaten to sweep him aside in the backwash of hopeless evolutionary superiority?

—Raymond F. Jones, "The Children's Room," 1962 short story

I think what we fear most about finding a mind equal to our own, but of another species, is that they will truly see us—and find us lacking, and turn away from us in disgust. That contact with another mind will puncture our species' self-satisfied feeling of worth. We will have to confront, finally, what we truly are, and the damage we have done to our home.

—Ray Naylor, *The Mountain in the Sea*, 2022 novel

The test of life is, "Can an advanced lifeform make it to another planet before it destroys itself?" Most advanced life fails. That's why we never encounter any other civilizations.

—Heather Anne Campbell and Glen Morgan, "Six Degrees of Freedom," 2019 episode of *The Twilight Zone*

They might have seventeen biological sexes, for all I know. Or none. No one ever talks about the really hard parts of first contact with intelligent alien life: pronouns.

—**Andy Weir,** *Project Hail Mary,* **2021 novel**

But am I going to risk the possible future of the human race on a guess that it's safe to trust them? God knows it would be worthwhile to make friends with a new civilization! It would be bound to stimulate our own, and maybe we'd gain enormously. But I can't take chances.

—**Murray Leinster, "First Contact," 1945 short story**

FREEDOM

The surest way to tame a prisoner is to let him believe he is free.
> —Anna Ouyang Moench, "The Grim Barbarity
> of Optics and Design," 2022 episode of *Severance*

Quite an experience to live in fear, isn't it? That's what it is to be a slave.
> —Hampton Fancher and David Peoples, *Blade Runner*, 1982 film

Is the prisoner a prisoner because he lives in a cage or because he knows that he lives in a cage?
> —Michael Moorcock, *The Dancers at the End of Time*, 1981 novel

They want to be controlled. They crave the comfort of certainty.
> —Lana Wachowski, David Mitchell, and Aleksandar Hemon,
> *The Matrix Resurrections*, 2021 film

Once men turned their thinking over to machines in the hope that this would set them free. But that only permitted other men with machines to enslave them.
> —Frank Herbert, *Dune*, 1965 novel

The worst kind of prison is one without boundaries.
> —S. D. Unwin, *One Second per Second*, 2021 novel

What's the difference between a prison and a sanctuary? Perhaps it's merely a matter of perspective, or of the quality of the cage. A rhetorical question to be pondered from the comfort or the confines of your own.
> —Mark Rahner, *The Twilight Zone: Shadow and Substance*, 2015 comic

They think if people can possess enough things they will be content to live in prison.

—**Ursula K. Le Guin, *The Dispossessed*, 1974 novel**

Did we ever have more than that: the illusion of freedom?

—**Robert Silverberg, "Passengers," 1968 short story**

Long-established totalitarian governments fear any kind of free expression. A sculpture can be a manifesto, a manuscripted adventure can double as a cry for rebellion.

—**Alan Dean Foster, *Splinter of the Mind's Eye*, 1978 novel**

Freedom does that to people, he realizes. Once you've tasted it, you never want to let go.

—**Allen Steele, *Coyote*, 2002 novel**

I'd rather struggle and fail on my own than be coddled as a slave.

—**Christopher Paolini, *To Sleep in a Sea of Stars*, 2020 novel**

We cannot be free until we have power.

—**Paul Dehn, *Conquest of the Planet of the Apes*, 1972 film**

They have turned you into something other than a human being. You have no power of choice any longer. You are committed to socially acceptable acts, a little machine capable only of good.

—**Anthony Burgess, *A Clockwork Orange*, 1962 novel**

Freedom was wonderful beyond relief. But with it came that bitch, Duty.

—**David Brin, *The Postman*, 1985 novel**

Each man is his own prisoner, in solitary confinement for life.

—Robert A. Heinlein, *If This Goes On—***, 1940 novel**

Beyond a critical point within a finite space, freedom diminishes as numbers increase. This is true of humans in the infinite space of a planetary ecosystem as it is of gas molecules sealed in a flask.

—Frank Herbert, *Dune***, 1965 novel**

It came to him, with the force of a revelation, that you had to have been imprisoned to fully understand what freedom was.

—Stephen King, *The Institute***, 2019 novel**

Humans tended to use the terms free and freedom to indicate states of being that were anything but.

—Robert Repino, *Mort(e)***, 2015 novel**

A rat in a maze is free to go anywhere, as long as it stays inside the maze.

—Margaret Atwood, *The Handmaid's Tale***, 1985 novel**

FREE WILL

You are all sleepwalkers, whether climbing creative peaks or slogging through some mundane routine for the thousandth time. You are all sleepwalkers.

—Peter Watts, *Blindsight*, 2006 novel

Was all the world just a stage for a play already written?

—Matthew Mather, *The Dystopia Chronicles*, 2014 novel

The brain is a soupy lightning storm swirling and crackling in three pounds of wet meat. Do conscious decisions even exist, or is everything an instinctual response gussied up with malformed logic?

—Elan Mastai, *All Our Wrong Todays*, 2017 novel

The illusion of self-awareness. Happy automatons, running on trivial programs. I'll bet you never guess. From the inside, how can you?

—Vernor Vinge, *A Fire upon the Deep*, 1992 novel

You don't have free will, David. You have the appearance of free will.

—George Nolfi, *The Adjustment Bureau*, 2011 film

One acts, and thus finds out what one has decided to do.

—Kim Stanley Robinson, *Aurora*, 2015 novel

The future isn't quite clear, like the past. There's a dark cloud moves across the spectral lines and blurs them. I think it's the element of free will—or God!

—Victor Rousseau, "The Atom Smasher," 1930 short story

The future has not been written. There is no fate but what we make for ourselves. I wish I could believe that.

—**John Brancato and Michael Ferris,**
***Terminator 3: Rise of the Machines*, 2003 film**

We are born; we choose neither our parents, nor our station; we are educated by others, or by the world's circumstance, and this cultivation, mingling with our innate disposition, is the soil in which our desires, passions, and motives grow.

—**Mary Shelley, *The Last Man*, 1826 novel**

Does it really matter if there's no such thing as free will?

—**David Gerrold, *The Man Who Folded Himself*, 1973 novel**

Today is the result of yesterday's probabilities, and tomorrow will materialize from today's.

—**Douglas Phillips, *Quantum Void*, 2018 novel**

He had the dim realization that the universe, like a huge sleepy animal, knew what he was trying to do and was trying to thwart him.

—**Fritz Leiber, "Try and Change the Past," 1958 short story**

There's a cosmic flowchart that dictates where you can and where you can't go. I've given you the knowledge. I've set you free.

—**Charlie Brooker, *Black Mirror: Bandersnatch*, 2018 film**

My message to you is this: pretend that you have free will. It's essential that you behave as if your decisions matter, even though you know that they don't. The reality isn't important: what's important is your belief, and believing the lie is the only way to avoid a waking coma.

—**Ted Chiang, "What's Expected of Us," 2005 short story**

THE FUTURE

How can you expect to handle the future if you can't even handle the present?
—Daniel Suarez, *Daemon*, 2006 novel

We were making the future, and hardly any of us troubled to think what future we were making.
—H. G. Wells, *When the Sleeper Wakes*, 1899 novel

We can grow up. We can leave the nest. We can fulfill the Destiny, make homes for ourselves among the stars, and become some combination of what we want to become and whatever our new environments challenge us to become.
—Octavia E. Butler, *Parable of the Talents*, 1998 novel

I was at what seemed the pinnacle of civilization, where mankind was resting and enjoying the results of its labors. Decadence was bound to come, as truly as death followed birth.
—Ray Cummings, *The Man Who Mastered Time*, 1929 novel

The very rich were investing in the space colony, and the regular rich were building solar-powered mansions in the coldest parts of the planet. The very poor were dead. The regular poor stayed alive any way they could, living on sugar and pills, playing on their phones indoors, a slow suicide.
—Edan Lepucki, "There's No Place Like Home," 2018 short story

The average span of a human generation is twenty-five years. Any reward occurring beyond this generational horizon creates an imbalance that undermines long-term cooperation. In short, we as a species are motivated to betray our own descendants.
—Daniel H. Wilson, *The Andromeda Evolution*, 2019 novel

But Earth would never die, for there was a part of Earth in every man and woman who would go forth into space, part of Earth's courage, part of Earth's ideals, part of Earth's dreams.

—Clifford D. Simak, *Empire*, 1951 novel

Your future hasn't been written yet. No one's has. Your future is whatever you make it. So make it a good one.

—Robert Zemeckis and Bob Gale, said by Doc Brown,
Back to the Future, 1985 film

This is the future. This is where mankind takes its next great step. This is where we become gods.

—Adrian Tchaikovsky, *Children of Time*, 2015 novel

Why is it always, always so costly for Man to move from the present to the future?

—Robert Creighton Williams, Charlotte Knight, and Christopher Knopf,
20 Million Miles to Earth, 1957 film

I believe that migration, friendship, commerce, even war, between the inhabitants of different planets of our solar system was intended by Almighty God—and, in good time, will come to pass.

—Ray Cummings, *The Fire People*, 1922 novel

Perhaps it is better to be un-sane and happy, than sane and un-happy. But it is the best of all to be sane and happy. Whether our descendants can achieve that goal will be the greatest challenge of the future. Indeed, it may well decide whether we have any future.

—Arthur C. Clarke, *3001: The Final Odyssey*, 1997 novel

I knew I was an Anachronic Man; my age was still to come.

—H. G. Wells, "The Chronic Argonauts," 1888 short story

Better to make a good future than predict a bad one.

—Isaac Asimov, *Prelude to Foundation*, 1988 novel

Difficult to see. Always in motion is the future.

—**Leigh Brackett and Lawrence Kasdan, said by Yoda,**
***Star Wars: Episode V—The Empire Strikes Back*, 1980 film**

Anyone who tries to predict the future is inevitably a fool.

—**David Brin, *Earth*, 1990 novel**

GODS, RELIGIONS, AND BELIEF

I'll never understand what possessed my mother to put her faith in God's hands, rather than her local geneticist.

—Andrew Niccol, *Gattaca*, **1997 film**

The universe is God's self-portrait.

—Octavia E. Butler, *Parable of the Sower*, **1993 novel**

"Which God," she asked. "There are such a lot of them."

—Aldous Huxley, *Island*, **1962 novel**

Man does not create gods, in spite of appearances. The times, the age, impose them on him.

—Stanislaw Lem, *Solaris*, **1961 novel**

It's alive! Oh, in the name of God! Now I know what it feels like to be God!

—Francis Edward Faragoh, Garrett Fort, Robert Florey, and John Russell, *Frankenstein*, **1931 film**

Religion was the creation of fear. Knowledge destroys fear. Without fear, religion can't survive.

—Michael Moorcock, *Behold the Man*, **1969 novel**

God's law, God's voice, God's words. It's amazing how they all just align with whatever it is that you want at any given moment.

—Steven Knight and Jonathan Tropper, "House of Enlightenment," 2019 episode of *See*

There exists no separation between gods and men; one blends softly casual into the other.

—**Frank Herbert,** *Dune Messiah,* **1969 novel**

One believes things because one has been conditioned to believe them.

—**Aldous Huxley,** *Brave New World,* **1932 novel**

I've always found that when people try to convince others of their beliefs it's because they're really just trying to convince themselves.

—**René Echevarria, "Covenant," 1998 episode of** *Star Trek: Deep Space Nine*

Every civilization has its ghosts. Usually they are the gods of the last one.

—**James Gunn,** *The Listeners,* **1972 novel**

One ape's hallucination is another ape's religious experience, it just depends on which one's god module is overactive at the time.

—**Charles Stross,** *Accelerando,* **2005 novel**

If you sincerely believed in God, how could you form one thought, speak one sentence, without mentioning Him?

—**Neal Stephenson,** *Anathem,* **2008 novel**

In another thousand years we'll be machines, or gods.

—**Bruce Sterling,** *Swarm,* **1982 novel**

Our gods are dead. Ancient Klingon warriors slew them a millennia ago. They were more trouble than they were worth.

—**Ira Steven Behr and Robert Hewitt Wolfe, said by Worf, "Homefront," 1996 episode of** *Star Trek: Deep Space Nine*

The human mind delights in grand visions of supernatural beings.
—Jules Verne, *Twenty Thousand Leagues under the Seas*, 1870 novel

Faith is a story of order humans impose on the chaos of their existence so their soft brains can bear it.
—Sam Vincent and Jonathan Brackley, season 3, episode 2 of *Humans*, 2018

Man's religion and metaphysics are the voices of his glands.
—Alice Sheldon (under the pseudonym Raccoona Sheldon), "The Screwfly Solution," 1977 short story

A civilization that cannot see the sun and stars will be without religion.
—Liu Cixin, "Mountain," 2006 short story

In times of desperation, people will believe what they want to believe.
—John Brancato and Michael Ferris, *Terminator: Salvation*, 2009 film

The characteristic human trait is not awareness but conformity, and the characteristic result is religious warfare. Other animals fight for territory or food; but, uniquely in the animal kingdom, human beings fight for their "beliefs."
—Michael Crichton, *The Lost World*, 1995 novel

Through the practice of faith, whatever its specific rituals, one brought into existence the object of that faith. The believer became the Creator.
—Nancy Kress, *Beggars in Spain*, 1993 novel

One man's theology is another man's belly laugh.
—Robert A. Heinlein, *Time Enough for Love*, 1973 novel

We don't choose the things we believe in. They choose us.

—**Scott Frank and Jon Cohen,** *Minority Report,* **2002 film**

Perhaps we shouldn't completely ignore the old beliefs no matter how strange they may seem today.

—**Scott Miller and Joe Menosky, "Blink of An Eye,"**
2000 episode of *Star Trek: Voyager*

We can create cybernetic individuals who, in just a few short years, will be completely indistinguishable from us. Which leads to an obvious conclusion: We are the gods now.

—**Jon Spaihts and Damon Lindelof,** *Prometheus,* **2012 film**

HAPPINESS

That was when I realized, as terrifying and painful as reality can be, it's also the only place where you can find true happiness. Because reality is real.

—**Ernest Cline, *Ready Player One*, 2011 novel**

We give them happiness and they give us authority.

—**Chris Carter, "Talithia Cumi," 1996 episode of *The X-Files***

We have everything we need to be happy, but we aren't happy. Something's missing.

—**Ray Bradbury, *Fahrenheit 451*, 1953 novel**

Our greatest challenge to achieving happiness is not the obstacles we encounter in our life. The true barrier to happiness lies inside of us—and it's the one thing we can't ever escape: our own mind.

—**A. G. Riddle, *The Extinction Trials*, 2021 novel**

Happiness doesn't breed creativity or ingenuity or invention. No, progress is borne out of a terrible struggle, a stew of agony and suffering.

—**Mercurio D. Rivera, "Beyond the Tattered Veil of Stars,"**
2020 short story

In my life, I have found two things of priceless worth—learning and loving. Nothing else—not fame, not power, not an achievement for its own sake—can possibly have the same lasting value. For when your life is over if you can say "I have learned" and "I have loved," you will also be able to say "I have been happy."

—**Arthur C. Clarke and Gentry Lee, *Rama II*, 1989 novel**

But there are no happy endings. There are no endings of any kind. At most, we are given happy moments.

—**Poul Anderson,** *There Will Be Time,* **1972 novel**

Quit worrying and enjoy the ride.

—**Robert A. Heinlein,** *The Number of the Beast,* **1980 novel**

HATE AND ANGER

What you fail to understand is the power of hate. It can fill the heart as surely as love can.

—Earl Felton, said by Captain Nemo,
20,000 Leagues under the Sea, 1954 film

Nobody can hate Man more than Man.

—Karel Čapek, *R.U.R.*, 1920 play,
translated by Paul Selver and Nigel Playfair

Whoever we dislike, are there facts we could learn that would change our minds?

—Richard Bach, *One*, 1988 novel

Being truly intelligent, he hated nothing.

—Abraham Grace Merritt, "The Last Poet and the Robots,"
1936 short story

Anger is more useful than despair.

—John Brancato and Michael Ferris, *Terminator 3:
Rise of the Machines*, 2003 film

You can't hate a man you understand.

—Ben Bova, *Return to Mars*, 1999 novel

Let go of your hate.

—Lawrence Kasdan and George Lucas, said by Luke Skywalker,
Star Wars: Episode VI—Return of the Jedi, 1983 film

HISTORY

There are no happy endings in history, only crisis points that pass.
—**Isaac Asimov**, *The Gods Themselves*, 1972 novel

History was like some vast thing that was always over the tight horizon, invisible except in its effects. It was what happened when you weren't looking—an unknowable infinity of events, which although out of control, controlled everything.

—**Kim Stanley Robinson**, *Red Mars*, 1992 novel

I think perhaps of all the things a police state can do to its citizens, distorting history is possibly the most pernicious.

—**Robert A. Heinlein**, *If This Goes On—*, 1940 novel

The past is forbidden. Why? Because when we can cut man from his own past, then we can cut him from his family, his children, other men.

—**Michael Radford**, *1984*, 1984 film

Forget history, and you are doomed to repeat the mistakes of the past. Forget how bad polio was, people stop taking vaccines. Forget how bad world wars are, people start puffing out their chests.

—**Greg Daniels, "Proportionate Response,"**
2020 episode of *Space Force*

The past does not die; it seeps, leaks, infiltrates, waits for an opportunity to spring up.

—**Ken Liu, "The Reborn," 2014 short story**

What is remembered says a great deal about those doing the remembering.
—**Timothy Zahn**, *Thrawn: Star Wars*, 2017 novel

History is the ultimate weapon, because it harnesses time itself. Used correctly, the past can alter the present.
—**Victoria Morrow**, "The First Crisis," 2021 episode of *Foundation*

The only truly alien influence is the dead grasping fingers of our own past.
—**Charlie Jane Anders**, *The City in the Middle of the Night*, 2019 novel

"Who controls the past controls the future; who controls the present controls the past," repeated Winston obediently.
—**George Orwell**, *Nineteen Eighty-Four*, 1949 novel

This society—what we call modern society, what we always think of as the most important time the world has ever known, simply because we are in it—is just the sausage made by grinding up history.
—**Ray Naylor**, *The Mountain in the Sea*, 2022 novel

History, which interprets the past to understand the present and confront the future, is the least rewarding discipline for a dying species.
—**P. D. James**, *The Children of Men*, 1992 novel

History was written and rewritten so many times that the fabric of reality began to wear thin.
—**Jodi Taylor**, *Doing Time*, 2019 novel

HOPE

The world is full of painful stories. Sometimes it seems as though there aren't any other kind and yet I found myself thinking how beautiful that glint of water was through the trees.

—**Octavia E. Butler,** *Parable of the Sower,* 1993 novel

Hope is a gateway drug, don't do it.

—**Colson Whitehead,** *Zone One,* 2011 novel

I know everything feels hopeless to you in this moment, but this is just a moment, and moments pass.

—**Blake Crouch,** *Recursion,* 2019 novel

When I choose to see the good side of things, I'm not being naive. It is strategic and necessary. It's how I learned to survive through everything.

—**Daniel Kwan and Daniel Scheinert,**
Everything Everywhere All at Once, 2022 film

When there is no real hope we must mint our own.

—**Roger Zelazny,** *Lord of Light,* 1967 novel

Now I don't pretend to tell you how to find happiness and love, when every day is just a struggle to survive. But I do insist that you do survive. Because the days and the years ahead are worth living for.

—**Harlan Ellison, D. C. Fontana, and Gene L. Coon,**
"The City on the Edge of Forever," 1967 episode of *Star Trek*

Sometimes you just have to hold on, to keep doing what you're doing, to have faith that things are going to get better. It's how we survive.

—Alastair Reynolds, *House of Suns*, 2008 novel

A little hope is effective. A lot of hope is dangerous.

—Suzanne Collins, Gary Ross, and Billy Ray, *Hunger Games*, 2012 film

Hope. It is the quintessential human delusion, simultaneously the source of your greatest strength and your greatest weakness.

—Lana Wachowski and Lilly Wachowski, *The Matrix Reloaded*, 2003 film

Defect of my species. We never give up hope.

**—Brannon Braga and André Bormanis,
"Nothing Left on Earth Excepting Fishes," 2019 episode of *The Orville***

I dream with my eyes open.

—Jules Verne, *Journey to the Centre of the Earth*, 1864 novel

The promise of tomorrow. When today isn't working, tomorrow is what you have.

—Malorie Blackman and Chris Chibnall, "Rosa," 2018 episode of *Dr. Who*

I saw hope in the stars. It was stronger than fear, and I went towards it.

**—Bo Yeon Kim and Erika Lippoldt, "The Brightest Star,"
2018 episode of *Star Trek: Short Treks***

When I served under Leia, she always told me: "Hope is like the sun. If you only believe in it when you can see it, you'll never make it through the night."

—Rian Johnson, *Star Wars: Episode VIII—The Last Jedi*, 2019 film

I hope, or I could not live.

—**H. G. Wells,** *The Island of Doctor Moreau*, **1896 novel**

Resistance is not futile?

—**René Echevarria, "I, Borg," 1992 episode of**
Star Trek: The Next Generation

HUMANS

Shall I tell you what I find beautiful about you? You are at your very best when things are worst.

—**Bruce A. Evans, Raynold Gideon, and Dean Riesner,**
***Starman*, 1984 film**

But the most disturbing thing we found about humans is that, from a cellular standpoint, they are only half human. Fifty percent of their cells are symbiotic or parasitic microbial cells.

—**Kevin A. Kuh, "The Case against Humanity," 2020 short story**

Beware the beast man, for he is the Devil's pawn. Alone among God's primates, he kills for sport, or lust, or greed. Yea, he will murder his brother to possess his brother's land. Let him not breed in great numbers, for he will make a desert of his home and yours. Shun him. Drive him back into his jungle lair, for he is the harbinger of death.

—**Michael Wilson and Rod Serling,**
from the Lawgiver's Sacred Scrolls, *Planet of the Apes*, 1968 film

You're an interesting species. An interesting mix. You're capable of such beautiful dreams, and such horrible nightmares.

—**James V. Hart and Michael Goldenberg, *Contact*, 1997 film**

Would humanity be better if it was a little less human?

—**Peter Cawdron, *The Tempest*, 2022 novel**

The world changes, Larry, but not human nature.

—**Sewell Peaslee Wright, "The Man from 2071," 1931 short story**

Man. Big Daddy of the primates. The ape that walks like a chicken. Homo sap. Ah, the tool-maker, flapper of tongues, builder of fires, sex fiend, dreamer, destroyer, creator of garbage …

—Chad Oliver, *King of the Hill*, 1972 novel

Some believe what separates men from animals is our ability to reason. Others say it's language or romantic love, or opposable thumbs. Living here in this lost world, I've come to believe it is more than our biology. What truly makes us human is our unending search, our abiding desire for immortality.

—Arthur Conan Doyle, *The Lost World*, 1912 novel

Man adapts to the world, and the world adapts to man. The only thing man couldn't seem to adapt to was himself.

—Alan Dean Foster, *Cyber Way*, 1990 novel

You see, you human beings are a very paradoxical race. Greedy, but capable of acts of stunning selflessness; violent, but capable of turning your backs on war; splendid at love, but so talented at hate.

—Adam-Troy Castro, "Orientation," 2022 short story

I think we've underestimated the life on this planet. The people have so much courage. Here they are hurling through space on a molten rock at 67,000 miles an hour and the only thing that keeps them from flying out of their shoes is their misplaced faith in gravity.

—Bonnie Turner and Terry Turner, "Brains and Eggs,"
1996 episode of *3rd Rock from the Sun*

There is no gene for the human spirit.

—Columbia Pictures and Jersey Films, tagline, *Gattaca*, 1997 film

Slavery. Concentration camps. Interstellar wars. We have nothing in our past that approaches that kind of barbarism. You see? We're nothing like you. We're better.

—**Ira Steven Behr, said by Quark (extraterrestrial),**
"The Jem'Hadar," 1994 episode of *Star Trek: Deep Space Nine*

A human being takes a long time to grow, to mature, but it only takes a moment to damage and destroy him.

—**Philip K. Dick and Ray Nelson,** *The Ganymede Takeover,*
1967 novel

Technology advances, but humans don't. We're smart monkeys and what we want is always the same: food, shelter, sex and, in all its forms . . . escape.

—**Steve Blackman, "Fallen Angel," 2018 episode of** *Altered Carbon*

Improve a mechanical device and you may double productivity. But improve Man, you gain a thousandfold.

—**Gene L. Coon and Carey Wilber, "Space Seed,"**
1967 episode of *Star Trek*

"We are meat machines transporting slow genes into the future, while looking at the stars," he said—a reply he had used with many others. "Our genetic purpose is to live, to consume and to breed and there is nothing beyond that until the advent of higher mind."

—**Neal Asher, "Moral Biology," 2020 short story**

They were more cruel even than the apes who had preceded them, cruel with the utter cruelty of the mad. And in their progressive insanity they came to starve in the midst of plenty, to slay each other in their own cities, to cower beneath the lash of superstitious fears as no creatures had before them.

—**Edmund Hamilton, "Devolution," 1936 short story**

One moment there are these barefoot Neolithic hunters, bickering over a frozen caribou carcass. Turn around, and their children's children talk about tapping energy from pulsars.

—David Brin, *Earth*, 1990 novel

Only when we have to fight to stay human do we realize how precious it is to us, how dear.

—Daniel Mainwaring, *Invasion of the Body Snatchers*, 1956 film

We are a side-effect of the universe, not its central function—which seems to be to create star stuff, to form stars.

—Stephen Baxter, *The Thousand Earths*, 2022 novel

A man is something that feels happy, plays the piano, likes going for a walk, and, in fact, wants to do a whole lot of things that are really unnecessary.

**—Karel Čapek, *R.U.R.*, 1920 play,
translated by Paul Selver and Nigel Playfair**

The brief span of an individual life is misleading. Each one of us is as old as the entire biological kingdom, and our bloodstreams are tributaries of the great sea of its total memory.

—J. G. Ballard, *The Drowned World*, 1962 novel

Never listen to what people say. Just watch what they do.

—Mark Fergus and Hawk Ostby, "Safe," 2017 episode of *The Expanse*

As a species, we're fundamentally insane. Put more than two of us in a room, we pick sides and start dreaming up reasons to kill one another. Why do you think we invented politics and religion?

—Frank Darabont, *The Mist*, 2007 film

It's a miracle these people ever got out of the twentieth century.

—**Steve Meerson, Peter Krikes, Nicholas Meyer, and Harve Bennett,
said by Dr. Leonard McCoy,** *Star Trek IV: The Voyage Home*, **1986 film**

Monkeys, he thought, monkeys with a spot of poetry in them, cluttering and wasting a second-string planet near a third-string star. But sometimes they finish in style.

—**Robert A. Heinlein, "The Year of the Jackpot," 1952 short story**

In all the universe, can there be creatures more strange than the species called man?

—**Robert C. Dennis, "The Duplicate Man,"
1964 episode of** *The Outer Limits*

INTELLIGENCE

Intelligence is not a winning survival trait.

—Tim Miller and Philip Gelatt, "Swarm,"
2022 episode of *Love, Death + Robots*

Yet all the suns that light the corridors of the universe shine dim before the blazing of a single thought.

—Harry Kleiner, *Fantastic Voyage*, 1966 film

"Our intelligence becomes a more powerful thing every day," he continued. "We are growing dependent on it, and that may be our downfall. Who can know if the thing that destroys us someday is a thing we ourselves think up?"

—Steven R. Boyett, said by Zook (an Australopithecus in prehistoric
Africa), "Minutes of the Last Meeting at Olduvai," 1987 short story

Charles, I tell you brains will be the ruination of the human race.

—Harry Bates, "Alas All Thinking," 1935 short story

The world's been here for millions of years. Man's been walking upright for a comparatively short time. Mentally we're still crawling.

—Fred Freiberger, Eugène Lourié, Louis Morheim, and Robert Smith,
The Beast from 20,000 Fathoms, 1953 film

He often argued that human intelligence was more trouble than it was worth. It was more destructive than creative, more confusing than revealing, more discouraging than satisfying, more spiteful than charitable.

—Michael Crichton, *The Andromeda Strain*, 1969 novel

"It means," he explained, "that you cannot use a spear to kill a flea which is biting you, and a shield is no use against a monster that could gobble you up shield and all. There is only one way to win against both a flea and a monster: you must think better than either of them."

—**John Brunner**, *Stand on Zanzibar*,
1968 novel

His body often seemed absurd to him, a mere bag of meat and bone and blood and feces and miscellaneous ropes and cords and rags, sagging under time's assault, deteriorating from year to year and from hour to hour. What was noble about such a mound of protoplasm? The preposterousness of fingernails! The idiocy of nostrils! The foolishness of elbows! Yet under the armored skull ticked the watchful gray brain, like a bomb buried in mud.

—**Robert Silverberg**, *Tower of Glass*,
1970 novel

Fortune favors the brain, dude.

—**Travis Beacham and Guillermo del Toro**, *Pacific Rim*,
2013 film

We're not hunter-gatherers anymore. We're all living like patients in the intensive care unit of a hospital. What keeps us alive isn't bravery, or athleticism, or any of those other skills that were valuable in a caveman society. It's our ability to master complex technological skills. It is our ability to be nerds. We need to breed nerds.

—**Neal Stephenson**, *Seveneves*,
2015 novel

I grieved to think how brief the dream of the human intellect had been. It had committed suicide.

—**H. G. Wells**, *The Time Machine*,
1895 novel

I feel myself reaching that stage in the dim future of mankind when the mind will cast off the hamperings of the flesh and become all thought and no matter. A vortex of pure intelligence and space.

—**Ellis St. Joseph, "The Sixth Finger,"**
1963 episode of *The Outer Limits*

As far as we can see we're alone, in an indifferent universe. We see no sign of intelligence anywhere away from Earth. We may be the first. Perhaps we're the last.

—**Stephen Baxter,** *Manifold: Time*, **1999 novel**

JUSTICE

There are times, young fellah, when every one of us must make a stand for human right and justice, or you never feel clean again.
—**Arthur Conan Doyle,** *The Lost World,* 1912 novel

Prisons are needed only to provide the illusion that courts and police are effective.
—**Frank Herbert,** *God Emperor of Dune,* 1981 novel

The flower of justice is peace.
—**Ann Leckie,** *Ancillary Justice,* 2013 novel

Ethically and technologically, they were a million years ahead of humankind, for in unlocking the meaning of nature they had conquered even their baser selves, and, when in the course of eons, they had abolished sickness and insanity, crime and all injustice, they turned, still in high benevolence, upwards towards space.
—**Cyril Hume,** *Forbidden Planet,* 1956 film

Laws are confusing documents. They get in the way of justice.
—**Paolo Bacigalupi,** *The Windup Girl,* 2009 novel

There can be no justice so long as laws are absolute. Even life itself is an exercise in exceptions.
—**Worley Thorne,** "Justice," 1987 episode of
Star Trek: The Next Generation

KNOWLEDGE, IGNORANCE, AND LEARNING

Insufficient facts always invite danger.

—**Gene L. Coon and Carey Wilber, said by Spock,
"Space Seed," 1967 episode of** *Star Trek*

The admission of ignorance is the beginning of wisdom.

—**James Edwin Gunn,** *Transcendental***, 2013 novel**

We dive deep into the ocean of knowledge and try to find out the precious gems that Nature has kept in store for us.

—**Rokeya Sakhawat Hossain, "Sultana's Dream," 1905 short story**

I fear my ignorance.

—**Isaac Asimov,** *The Gods Themselves***, 1972 novel**

It's never a waste of time to educate others.

—**N. K. Jemisin,** *The Obelisk Gate***, 2016 novel**

The vast unknown of nature, so vast that everything which was real to me, understandable to me, was a mere drop in the ocean of the existing unknown.

—**Ray Cummings,** *Phantoms of Reality***, 1930 novel**

The search for knowledge is always our primary mission.

—**D. C. Fontana, "Lonely among Us,"
1987 episode of** *Star Trek: The Next Generation*

Half way up the sky, over the clustering roofs, chimneys and steeples of the city, hung the star. He looked at it as one might look into the eyes of a brave enemy. "You may kill me," he said after a silence. "But I can hold you—and all the universe for that matter—in the grip of this little brain."

—H. G. Wells, "The Star," 1897 short story

We make stupid mistakes when we're young; we do our best to make amends for them as we get older. We survive by learning; by learning we survive.

—Allen Steele, *Coyote*, 2002 novel

Because our minds process information almost solely through analogy and categorization, we are often defeated when presented with something that fits no category and lies outside of the realm of our analogies.

—Jeff VanderMeer, *Authority*, 2014 novel

It makes me uneasy to see the ignorance in which we run our world.

—George Zebrowski, *Macrolife: A Mobile Utopia*, 1979 novel

The most arduous part of learning is preparing the mind to accept new knowledge.

—Ben Bova, *New Earth*, 2013 novel

There's an abyss, okay? Sometimes I dream about it. It goes down forever, and it's full of all the things I don't know. I don't know how an abyss can be full—it's an oxymoron—but it is.

—Stephen King, *The Institute*, 2019 novel

I guess you could call it a "failure," but I prefer the term "learning experience."

—Andy Weir, *The Martian*, 2011 novel

It was idle to speculate, to build pyramids of surmise on a foundation of ignorance.
—**Arthur C. Clarke, *The City and the Stars*, 1956 novel**

We're blind moles. Creeping through the soil, feeling with our snoots. We know nothing.
—**Philip K. Dick, *The Man in the High Castle*, 1962 novel**

Ignorance was the enemy. Lies and superstition, misinformation, disinformation. Sometimes, no information at all. Ignorance killed billions of people. Ignorance caused the Zombie War.
—**Max Brooks, *World War Z: An Oral History of the Zombie War*, 2006 novel**

An easy life doesn't teach us anything.
—**Richard Bach, *One*, 1988 novel**

Information doesn't need topsoil to grow in, only freedom. Given eager minds and experimentation, it feeds itself like a chain reaction.
—**David Brin, *Earth*, 1990 novel**

Most ignorance is by choice, you know, and so ignorance is very telling about what really matters to people.
—**Kim Stanley Robinson, *Red Mars*, 1992 novel**

Your lack of understanding does not obligate me to explain.
—**Sarah Nolen, "The Missing Piece," 2021 episode of *Foundation***

That is the problem with ignorance. You can never truly know the extent of what you are ignorant about.
—**Adrian Tchaikovsky, *Children of Time*, 2015 novel**

Strange about learning; the farther I go the more I see that I never knew even existed. A short while ago I foolishly thought I could learn everything—all the knowledge in the world. Now I hope only to be able to know of its existence, and to understand one grain of it.

—**Daniel Keyes,** *Flowers for Algernon,* **1966 novel**

Learn all that is learnable.

—**Harold Livingston,** *Star Trek: The Motion Picture,* **1979 film**

LIFE

Life is the continuation of existence, yet no thing endures. We are all patterns, seeking to propagate. Patterns which bring other patterns into being, then vanish, as if we've never been.

—**David Brin,** ***Glory Season,*** **1993 novel**

Every life is paid for by some sacrifice.

—**Rick Remender,** ***Black Science:***
The Beginner's Guide to Entropy, **2016 comic**

Death can be senseless, but life never is.

—**Micaiah Johnson,** ***The Space between Worlds,*** **2020 novel**

To live is to risk it all. Otherwise, you're just an inert chunk of randomly assembled molecules drifting wherever the universe blows you.

—**Jane Becker, "Rickmancing the Stone,"**
2017 episode of ***Rick and Morty***

Across the sea of space lies an infinite emptiness. I can feel it, suffocating me. It is without meaning. But each *life* creates its own reality. And those realities are valuable beyond measure.

—**Daniel H. Wilson,** ***Robopocalypse,*** **2011 novel**

The cosmic process is hurrying on, crushing life back into the granite and methane; the wheel turns for all life. It is all temporary.

—**Philip K. Dick,** ***The Man in the High Castle,***
1962 novel

Humans, being intermediary creatures in both time and space, did not fully appreciate the value of life at every physical and temporal scale. Perhaps they never could.

—John Scalzi, "Slow Time between the Stars," 2023 short story

If you need something to worship, then worship life—all life, every last crawling bit of it! We're all in this beauty together!

—Frank Herbert, *Dune Messiah*, 1969 novel

Life itself is impossible, he thought, but men exist by reversing entropy.

—James Gunn, *The Listeners*, 1972 novel

Every species, every individual, is unique and should be evaluated as such.

—David A. Goodman, "From Unknown Graves,"
2022 episode of *The Orville*

Just because we don't understand a life form, doesn't mean we can destroy it.

—Jim Trombetta and Michael Piller, "Playing God,"
1994 episode of *Star Trek: Deep Space Nine*

We've just begun to learn about the water and its secrets, just as we've only touched on outer space. We don't entirely rule out the possibility that there might be some form of life on another planet, and why not some entirely different form of life in a world we already know is inhabited by millions of living creatures?

—Harry Essex and Arthur Ross, *Creature from the Black Lagoon*,
1954 film

Life's very existence requires destruction.

—Rhett Reese and Paul Wernick, *Life*, 2017 film

The Old Ones knew that life is not rare, but precious; not fragile, but vulnerable.

—**Ben Bova,** *Mars Life,* **2008 novel**

Time not important. Only life important.

—**Luc Besson and Robert Mark Kamen,** *The Fifth Element,* **1997 film**

Luminous beings are we. Not this crude matter.

—**Leigh Brackett and Lawrence Kasdan, said by Yoda,**
Star Wars: Episode V—The Empire Strikes Back, **1980 film**

You talk about life like it can't be manufactured.

—**Sam Vincent and Jonathan Brackley, season 1,**
episode 3 of *Humans,* **2015**

Life sometimes seems destined, to we fortunate ones who live at the far end of time's telescope. But what were the chances of success? Hard to say, and the no man's land between inorganic process and organic existence is a region, not a hard dividing line.

—**Adrian Tchaikovsky,** *The Doors of Eden,* **2020 novel**

Now we know why we couldn't find life in the universe. Turns out it's everywhere. The stars, the whole cosmos, is alive. We just couldn't see it.

—**Stephen Baxter,** *The Thousand Earths,* **2022 novel**

I'm simply saying that life finds a way.

—**Michael Crichton and David Koepp, said by Dr. Ian Malcolm,**
Jurassic Park, **1993 film**

LONELINESS AND SOLITUDE

An overcrowded world is the ideal place in which to be lonely.
—Brian Aldiss, "Super-Toys Last All Summer Long," 1969 short story

If one's different, one's bound to be lonely.
—Aldous Huxley, *Brave New World*, 1932 novel

Alone, bad. Friend, good!
—William Hurlbut, said by the Monster, *Bride of Frankenstein*, 1935 film

At the end of time, a moment will come when just one man remains. Then the moment will pass. Man will be gone. There will be nothing to show that we were ever here, but stardust. The last man, alone with God.
—Alex Garland, *Sunshine*, 2007 film

You see, we can feed the stomach with concentrates. We can supply microfilm for reading, recreation, even movies of a sort. We can pump oxygen in and waste material out. But there's one thing we can't simulate that's a very basic need: Man's hunger for companionship.
—Rod Serling, "Where Is Everybody?" 1959 episode of *The Twilight Zone*

Solitude, isolation are painful things, and beyond human endurance.
—Jules Verne, *The Mysterious Island*, 1875 novel

You can only get so far without a tribe.
**—Jon Favreau, "Chapter 4: The Gathering Storm,"
2022 episode of *The Book of Boba Fett***

At times I suffer from the strangest sense of detachment from myself and the world about me; I seem to watch it all from the outside, from somewhere inconceivably remote, out of time, out of space, out of the stress and tragedy of it all.

—**H. G. Wells,** *The War of the Worlds,* **1898 novel**

Was Robinson Crusoe ever lonelier than I feel, here in the big city, imprisoned by electronic disdain?

—**David Brin, "Insistence of Vision," 2013 short story**

If humans have this need for companionship, why are they also ashamed to admit it?

—**Barry B. Longyear,** *Enemy Mine,* **1980 novel**

Little and alone and afraid, he was utterly, absolutely insignificant. Millions upon millions of stars swam out there in the sea of space, more than he could ever see, more than he could imagine. They mocked his tiny dreams . . .

—**Chad Oliver, "Field Expedient," 1948 short story**

That's what death is, the great loneliness.

—**Philip K. Dick,** *Flow, My Tears, the Policeman Said,* **1974 novel**

A man, he told himself, must belong to something, must have some loyalty and some identity. The galaxy was too big a place for any being to stand naked and alone.

—**Clifford D. Simak,** *Way Station,* **1963 novel**

Most of us spend our entire lives in hiding.

—**James Gray and Ethan Gross,** *Ad Astra,* **2019 film**

No human is an island. They are rarely even peninsulas. There is a reason why one of the greatest punishments of humanity is to be placed in a solitary confinement, even for a short time. Being alone is another thing to remind them of death, a condition in which there is no one else and will be no one else again, ever.

—John Scalzi, "Slow Time between the Stars," 2023 short story

In my loneliness I decided that if I could not inspire love, which was my deepest hope, I would instead cause fear!

—Gene Wilder and Mel Brooks, said by the Monster,
***Young Frankenstein*, 1974 film**

The distances between the stars seem brief by contrast to the distances between each of us and his fellows.

—Thomas M. Disch, "Things Lost," 1972 short story

LOVE

If we have souls, they are made of the love we share. Undimmed by time and unbound by death.

—**Karl Gajdusek and Michael DeBruyn,** *Oblivion,* **2013 film**

Molecules trick each other into making more molecules and you call it Love.

—**Peter Watts, "Kindred," 2018 short story**

It is not that love sometimes makes mistakes, but that it is, essentially, a mistake. We fall in love when our imagination projects nonexistent perfections on to another person.

—**Samuel R. Delany,** *The Einstein Intersection,* **1967 novel**

It is remarkable how similar the pattern of love is to the pattern of insanity.

—**Lana Wachowski and Lilly Wachowski,** *The Matrix Revolutions,* **2003 film**

Yes, I was a fool, but I was in love, and though I was suffering the greatest misery I had ever known I would not have had it otherwise for all the riches of Barsoom. Such is love, and such are lovers wherever love is known.

—**Edgar Rice Burroughs,** *A Princess of Mars,* **1917 novel**

"Well, you can't love everything equally," she said. "You just can't—and if you did, then it's the same as loving nothing at all. So you have to hold just a few things dear, because that's what love is. Particular. Specific."

—**Veronica Roth,** *Ark,* **2019 novel**

There is no intimacy without consequence.

—**Elan Mastai,** *All Our Wrong Todays,* **2017 novel**

Love quiets fear.

—**Octavia E. Butler,** *Parable of Talents,* **1998 novel**

To love someone when there was nothing to be got from that person; that was love.

—**James Matheson,** *The Incredible Shrinking Man,* **1956 novel**

But what is grief, if not love persevering?

—**Laura Donney, "Previously On," 2021 episode of** *WandaVision*

I love you with every cell, with every atom. I love you on a subatomic level.

—**John Hughes,** *Flubber,* **1997 film**

We were human machines in a machine world. That was when the trouble began, when love vanished.

—*Weird Science,* **"A New Beginning," issue 22, 1953 comic**

There are worlds beyond and worlds within which the explorer must explore, but there is one power which seems to transcend space and time, life and death. It is a deeply human power which holds us safe and together when all other forces combine to tear us apart. We call it the power of love.

—**Leslie Stevens, "The Borderland," 1963 episode of** *The Outer Limits*

"This," I thought, "is power! Not to be strong of limb, hard of heart, ferocious, and daring; but kind, compassionate and soft."

—**Mary Shelley,** *The Last Man,* **1826 novel**

Perhaps one did not want to be loved so much as to be understood.

—**George Orwell,** *Nineteen Eighty-Four,* **1949 novel**

Listen, Morty, I hate to break it to you, but what people call "love" is just a chemical reaction that compels animals to breed. It hits hard, Morty, then it slowly fades, leaving you stranded in a failing marriage. I did it. Your parents are gonna do it. Break the cycle, Morty. Rise above. Focus on science.

—**Justin Roiland, "Rick Potion #9," 2014 episode of** *Rick and Morty*

To all mankind, may we never find space so vast, planets so cold, heart and mind so empty that we cannot fill them with love and warmth.

—**S. Bar-David, "Dagger of the Mind," 1966 episode of** *Star Trek*

She had studied the universe all her life, but had overlooked its clearest message: For small creatures such as we the vastness is bearable only through love.

—**Carl Sagan,** *Contact,* **1985 novel**

There is no such thing as time or distance, when measured in devotion.

—**Kai Hudson, "A Star for Every Word Unspoken," 2021 short story**

We must love what has been damaged, because everything has been damaged.

—**Jeff VanderMeer,** *Hummingbird Salamander,* **2021 novel**

I love you. I love you. I love you. I'll write it in waves. In skies. In my heart. You'll never see, but you will know. I'll be all the poets, I'll kill them all and take each one's place in turn, and every time love's written in all the strands it will be to you.

—**Amal El-Mohtar and Max Gladstone,**
This Is How You Lose the Time War, **2019 novel**

Don't ever be afraid of telling someone you love them. There are things wrong with your world, but an excess of love is not one.

—**Matt Haig,** *The Humans,* **2013 novel**

That's how we're gonna win. Not fighting what we hate, saving what we love.
    —Rian Johnson, *Star Wars: Episode VIII—The Last Jedi*, 2019 film

It is a feeling that cannot be quantified because it is not a number. Love is a pattern in the chaos.
    —**Daniel H. Wilson, "The Blue Afternoon That Lasted Forever,"**
    2014 short story

MEANING AND PURPOSE

What matters most is life itself. And the greatest thing about life is not having a purpose; it's about finding a purpose.

—**Bob Kushell, "Father Knows Dick,"**
1996 episode of *3rd Rock from the Sun*

The existentialists did say that life was all about pulling the victory of meaning from the jaws of senseless absurdity, and in that I'd discovered a purpose I'd struggled to find before.

—**Matthew Mather, *The Atopia Chronicles*, 2014 novel**

The mystery of life isn't a problem to solve, but a reality to experience.

—**Frank Herbert, *Dune*, 1965 novel**

By the time you're my age, you'll realize that everything you once thought mattered so much turns out to mean very little.

—**Liu Cixin, *The Three-Body Problem*, 2014 novel**

You exist to continue your existence. What's the point?

—**Kurt Wimmer, *Equilibrium*, 2002 film**

A father protects. It's what gives him meaning.

—**James Cameron, Rick Jaffa, and Amanda Silver,**
***Avatar: The Way of Water*, 2022 film**

A life that seems small on the outside can be limitless on the inside.

—**John Jackson Miller, *Kenobi*, 2013 novel**

Endure pain, find joy, and make your own meaning, because the universe certainly isn't going to supply it.

—**Lois McMaster Bujold,** *Barrayar*, **1991 novel**

You wanna know what I think your purpose is? It's obvious. You're here, along with the rest of us, to speed the entropic death of this planet. To service the chaos. We're maggots eating a corpse.

—**Suzanne Wrubel and Lisa Joy, "Decoherence,"**
2020 episode of *Westworld*

You have many years to live—do things you will be proud to remember when you're old.

—**John Brunner,** *Stand on Zanzibar*, **1968 novel**

There was no single meaning of life—there was only the meaning of your life.

—**A. G. Riddle,** *Lost in Time*, **2022 novel**

When you know nothing matters, the universe is yours.

—**Michael McMahan, "The ABCs of Beth,"**
2017 episode of *Rick and Morty*

Listen: We are here on Earth to fart around. Don't let anybody tell you any different!

—**Kurt Vonnegut,** *Timequake*, **1997 novel**

NATURE

The troubles of modern life come from being divorced from nature.

—Isaac Asimov, *The Caves of Steel*, 1954 novel

An ecosystem leaning on itself into a structure so magnificent that it can never be fully understood is a force so great that it both tears and lifts me.

—Hank Green, "A Naturalist on Hoth," 2020 short story

Heaven was a lovely, unspoiled Earth-like world; what Earth might have been like if men had treated her with compassion instead of lust.

—Joe Haldeman, *The Forever War*, 1974 novel

Nature knows when to give up, David.

—Lawrence Lasker and Walter F. Parkes, *WarGames*, 1983 film

Are we not natural creatures? Are we not evolved, too? Surely all the lessons we've learned in the past century come to a single point: we have to stop thinking of ourselves as somehow apart from nature, and recognize that we're inseparable from it.

—John Brunner, *The Stone That Never Came Down*, 1973 novel

Supernatural. Stupid word. Everything that happens, happens within nature, whether we believe it or not.

—Jerome Bixby, *The Man from Earth*, 2007 film

Without the group, without the tree, without the earth, no pattern guided them.

—Brian Aldiss, *Hothouse*, 1960 novel

Never give children a chance of imagining that anything exists in isolation. Make it plain from the very first that all living is relationship.

—**Aldous Huxley,** *Island*, **1962 novel**

You treat the world as you treat each other.

—**David Scarpa,** *The Day the Earth Stood Still*, **2008 film**

It was surely well for man that he came late in the order of creation.

—**Arthur Conan Doyle,** *The Lost World*, **1912 novel**

The belief that the world is here for humans to control is the philosophical bedrock of our civilization, but it's a mistaken belief.

—**Elan Mastai,** *All Our Wrong Todays*, **2017 novel**

Nothing in nature is terrifying when one understands it.

—**Willis Cooper,** *Son of Frankenstein*, **1939 film**

On this first day of a new century, we humbly beg forgiveness, and dedicate these last forests of our once-beautiful nation, in the hope that they will one day return and grace our fouled Earth. Until that day, may God bless these forests, and the brave men who care for them.

—**Deric Washburn, Michael Cimino, and Steven Bochco,**
Silent Running, **1972 film**

He needed sun and soil and wind to remain a man.

—**Clifford D. Simak,** *Way Station*, **1963 novel**

Humans succeed only because they have been given a perfect world.

—**Kevin A. Kuhn, "The Case against Humanity," 2020 short story**

But as the natural systems of the planet broke down, humans would discover conclusively that they were still, after all, just animals embedded in an eco-system; and as it died back, so did they.

—**Stephen Baxter,** *Evolution,* **2003 novel**

Sharing the world has never been humanity's defining attribute.

—**Michael Dougherty, Dan Harris, and David Hayter,**
X2: X-Men United, **2003 film**

And I wonder, in my last moments, if the planet does not mind that we wound her surface or pillage her bounty, because she knows we silly warm things are not even a breath in her cosmic life.

—**Pierce Brown,** *Morning Star,* **2016 novel**

We can't save the world without food. Only people with full stomachs become environmentalists.

—**David Brin,** *Earth,* **1990 novel**

It's not a good look to go off searching for life elsewhere while sterilizing your own planet.

—**Peter Cawdron,** *Déjà Vu,* **2021 novel**

Climate is the most potent factor of all that influences mankind.

—**Ray Cummings,** *The Man Who Mastered Time,* **1929 novel**

I never thought about how important the sky was until I didn't have one.

—**Beth Revis,** *Across the Universe,* **2011 novel**

There are many who are uncomfortable with what we have created. It is almost a biological rebellion. A profound revulsion against the planned communities. The programming. The sterilized, artfully balanced atmospheres. They hunger for an Eden where spring comes.

—**Arthur Heinemann, "The Way to Eden," 1969 episode of _Star Trek_**

People were always rotten. But the world was beautiful.

—**Stanley R. Greenberg, _Soylent Green_, 1973 film**

Our relationship with other species doesn't have to be a battle. Symbiosis is a much more powerful agent of change, and a much more successful one.

—**David Walton, _The Genius Plague_, 2017 novel**

Whatever your belief system, if life matters, you cannot single out one species and say that particular one does not matter. They all matter.

—**James Lawrence Powell, _The 2084 Report: A Novel of the Great Warming_, 2011 novel**

They say the water used to be so blue you could see it from space.

—**Wesley Chu, _Time Salvager_, 2015 novel**

Must Nature always be asked to straighten out the mess that man has made?

—**Karel Čapek, _War with the Newts_, 1936 novel**

The truth is that we've never, ever been independent, in terms of our survival. Plants, animals, the sun—we're leaning on a lot to get through the day.

—**David Harris Ebenbach, _How to Mars_, 2021 novel**

Do you realize that you will not only wreck your civilization, such as it is, and kill most of your people; but that you will also poison the fish in your rivers, the squirrels in your trees, the flocks of birds, the soil, the water? There are times when you seem, to us, like apes loose in a museum, carrying knives, slashing the canvases, breaking the statuary with hammers.

—**Walter Tevis,** *The Man Who Fell to Earth*, **1963 novel**

We are nature. Our every tinkering is nature, our every biological striving. We are what we are, and the world is ours. We are its gods.

—**Paolo Bacigalupi,** *The Windup Girl*, **2009 novel**

We consume and excrete, use and destroy. Then we sit here on a neat little pile of ashes, having squeezed anything of value out of this planet, and we ask ourselves, "Why are we here?"

—**Suzanne Wrubel and Lisa Joy, "Decoherence,"
2020 episode of** *Westworld*

Ecocide officially became a core international crime in 2050.

—**Dorothy Fortenberry, Diane Ademu-John, Scott Z. Burns,
and Ron Currie, "2070: Ecocide," 2023 episode of** *Extrapolations*

It is because nature is ruthless, hideous, and cruel beyond belief that it was necessary to invent civilisation.

—**John Wyndham,** *The Midwich Cuckoos*, **1957 novel**

One time we had the whole world in our hands, but we ate it and burned it and it's gone now.

—**Harry Harrison,** *Make Room! Make Room!* **1966 novel**

We may brave human laws, but we cannot resist natural ones.

—**Jules Verne,** *Twenty Thousand Leagues under the Seas*, **1870 novel**

Mother Nature is a serial killer. No one's better, more creative.

—**Matthew Michael Carnahan, Drew Goddard,
and Damon Lindelof,** *World War Z,* **2013 film**

Placing my hand against the black bark of the tree, I considered all the pro-
cesses—biological, chemical, evolutionary—that had brought it into existence.
It seemed, suddenly, to be the most marvelous thing I had ever seen.

—**Una McCormack, said by Spock,**
The Autobiography of Mr. Spock, **2021 novel**

We didn't even get as far as counting all the species before destroying them.

—**Stephen Baxter,** *Manifold: Time,* **1999 novel**

You talk as if cities were these self-supporting bubbles, but they're not. They're
entirely dependent on the natural world around them.

—**Matthew Mather,** *CyberStorm,* **2013 novel**

Men go and come, but Earth abides.

—**George R. Stewart,** *Earth Abides,* **1949 novel**

PEACE

How then to enforce peace? Not by reason, certainly, nor by education. If a man could not look at the fact of peace and the fact of war and choose the former in preference to the latter, what additional argument could persuade him?

—Isaac Asimov, *The Currents of Space*, 1952 novel

What greater source of peace exists than our ability to love our enemy?

—Lisa Randolph, "The War Without, the War Within,"
2018 episode of *Star Trek: Discovery*

You know, we give ourselves a bad rep, but we're genuinely empathetic as a species. I mean, we don't actually really want to kill each other.

—Charlie Brooker, "Men against Fire," 2016 episode of *Black Mirror*

We're human beings with the blood of a million savage years on our hands. But we can stop it. We can admit that we're killers, but we're not going to kill today. That's all it takes, knowing that we're not going to kill today.

—Gene L. Coon and Robert Hamner, said by James T. Kirk,
"A Taste of Armageddon," 1967 episode of *Star Trek*

We have encountered no hostile starfaring races. Conflict between different species is impractical. Peaceful trade and cultural exchange is preferable to war or invasion.

—Allen Steele, "Day of the Bookworm," 2017 short story

Every once in a while, declare peace. It confuses the hell out of your enemies.

—Ira Steven Behr, "The Homecoming,"
1993 episode of *Star Trek: Deep Space Nine*

When in doubt, don't kill anyone.

—**Annalee Newitz,** *The Terraformers,* **2023 novel**

Peace is a struggle against our very nature. A skin we stretch over the bone, muscle, and sinew of our own innate savagery.

—**Steve Blackman, "Fallen Angel," 2018 episode of** *Altered Carbon*

War is good for business.
Peace is good for business.

—**David S. Cohen and Martin A. Winer, thirty-fourth and thirty-fifth Ferengi Rules of Acquisition, "Destiny," 1995 episode of** *Star Trek: Deep Space Nine*

That's what peace is, right? Postponing the conflict until the thing you were fighting over doesn't matter.

—**James S. A. Corey, "Drive," 2012 short story**

No kill I.

—**Gene L. Coon, "Devil in the Dark," 1967 episode of** *Star Trek*

PHILOSOPHY

Our existence is a mere point, our lifespan an instant, our planet a mere atom.

—Voltaire, *Micromégas*, 1752 novel

From now on I will be a citizen—a citizen of no country but that bounded by the limits of my own mind.

—James Blish, *A Case of Conscience*, 1958 novel

We're only different from the bacteria because we are able to ask what the hell this is all about. Not answer, just ask.

—Carolyn Ives, "Umbernight," 2018 short story

Know yourself. You are worth knowing.

—Jo Walton, *The Just City*, 2015 novel

We call ourselves the wise ones, but what would a true *Homo sapiens* be like? What would he do? Surely it would first of all treasure its world, or worlds. It would look to the skies for other sapient lifeforms. And it would look to the universe as a whole.

—Terry Pratchett and Stephen Baxter, *The Long Cosmos*, 2016 novel

If you turn into a monster, is it still you inside?

—Craig Mazin, "Endure and Survive," 2023 episode of *The Last of Us*

You are what you do.

—Ronald Shusett, Dan O'Bannon, and Gary Goldman, *Total Recall*, 1990 film

My understanding transcends all possibilities of this universe. I do not need to know this universe because I possess this universe as a direct experience.

—**Frank Herbert, *Destination: Void*, 1966 novel**

From cradle to grave, everything we do is motivated by the need to answer one question: Who am I.

—**Ken Liu, "Dispatches from the Cradle: The Hermit— Forty-Eight Hours in the Sea of Massachusetts," 2016 short story**

We're all just wandering through the tundra of our existence, assigning value to worthlessness, when all that we love and hate, all we believe in and fight for and kill for and die for is as meaningless as images projected onto Plexiglass.

—**Blake Crouch, *Dark Matter*, 2016 novel**

Understanding of self is the beginning of understanding of the entire universe.

—**Isaac Asimov and Robert Silverberg, *The Positronic Man*, 1992 novel**

No man is obsolete.

—**Rod Serling, "The Obsolete Man," 1961 episode of *The Twilight Zone***

Is it stealing if it's already stolen?

—**Andrew Niccol, *In Time*, 2011 film**

Why are we born needing impossible things? Why is it that we all have things we need to live that simply do not exist in the universe? A purpose in life. Unconditional love? Our emotional needs met? Ha.

—**Elizabeth Bear, *Machine*, 2020 novel**

You are here for but an instant, and you mustn't take yourself too seriously.

—**Edgar Rice Burroughs,** *The Land That Time Forgot,*
1924 novel

Anyway, that's what life is, just one learning experience after another, and when you're through with all the learning experiences you graduate and what you get for a diploma is, you die.

—**Frederik Pohl,** *Gateway,* **1977 novel**

Life doesn't have to be something that just happens to us.

—**Matt Lieberman and Zak Penn,** *Free Guy,* **2021 film**

Travel far enough, you meet yourself.

—**David Mitchell,** *Cloud Atlas,* **2004 novel**

Is a man who chooses the bad perhaps in some ways better than a man who has the good imposed upon him?

—**Anthony Burgess,** *A Clockwork Orange,* **1962 novel**

Nobody exists on purpose. Nobody belongs anywhere. We're all going to die. Come watch TV.

—**Tom Kauffman and Justin Roiland, "Rixty Minutes,"**
2014 episode of *Rick and Morty*

I've been condemned to live.

—**Bill Baer, Bruno Lawrence, and Sam Pillsbury,**
The Quiet Earth, **1985 film**

The distance between individual stars is so huge that it is possible for one galaxy to slip through another galaxy without a collision between any of the billions of stars involved. And you're worried about returning a late library book.

—**Eric Idle,** *The Road to Mars,* **1999 novel**

You cannot destroy an idea!

—**Ira Steven Behr and Hans Beimler, "Far beyond the Stars,"**
1998 episode of *Star Trek: Deep Space Nine*

"Cynic" is a word invented by optimists to criticize realists.

—**Gregory Benford,** *In the Ocean of Night,* **1977 novel**

There comes a time when you look into the mirror, and you realize that what you see is all that you will ever be. Then you accept it. Or you kill yourself. Or you stop looking into mirrors.

—**J. Michael Straczynski, "Chrysalis," 1994 episode of** *Babylon 5*

As long as you don't choose, everything remains possible.

—**Jaco Van Dormael,** *Mr. Nobody,* **2009 film**

I'm not a kind of froth on the surface of the universe. I am the universe.

—**Stephen Baxter,** *Manifold: Time,* **1999 novel**

What is beauty, or goodness, or art, or love, or God? We are forever teetering on the brink of the unknowable, and trying to understand what can't be understood.

—**Isaac Asimov,** *The Caves of Steel,* **1954 novel**

So all in all there wasn't anything really wrong with my life. Except that, like most everyone else's I knew about, it had a big gaping hole in it, an enormous emptiness, and I didn't know how to fill it or even know what belonged there.

—**Jack Finney**, *Time and Again*, **1970 novel**

No serious philosophical problem is ever settled.

—**Arthur C. Clarke**, *The Songs of Distant Earth*, **1986 novel**

PREJUDICE

Why fight two upstart kingdoms when you can exploit their racial animus and have them fight each other?
—**David S. Goyer, "The Leap," 2021 episode of** *Foundation*

You can sway a thousand men by appealing to their prejudices quicker than you can convince one man by logic.
—**Robert A. Heinlein,** *Revolt in 2100,* **1953 novel**

You mean, people killed people, just because they were different from each other? That's disgusting.
—**Charles Woodgrove, "The Rules of Luton," 1976 episode of** *Space 1999*

A circle looks at a square and sees a badly made circle.
—**Jeff VanderMeer,** *Authority,* **2014 novel**

It's been my experience that the prejudices people feel about each other disappear when they get to know each other.
—**John Meredyth Lucas, said by James T. Kirk,**
"Elaan of Troyius," 1968 episode of *Star Trek*

I belonged to a new underclass, no longer determined by social status or the color of your skin. No, we now have discrimination down to a science.
—**Andrew Niccol,** *Gattaca,* **1997 film**

She learned quickly that it was not good to be too different. Great differences caused envy, suspicion, fear, charges of witchcraft.
—**Octavia E. Butler,** *Wild Seed,* **1980 novel**

The lies that come preinstalled. *My child is more important than yours. My tribe is more important than yours. My bloodline is the most important thing in the universe.* They poison everything you perceive, every thought you think.

—**Peter Watts, "Kindred," 2018 short story**

You're obsessed with skin. Skin is one of your gods. You've created cults around it. Commit genocide. Murder every day in its name.

—**Jane Maggs, Jenny Lumet, and Alex Kurtzman,**
"As the World Falls Down," 2022 episode of
The Man Who Fell to Earth

We're one species, with one future. It doesn't matter if we like each other or not; we still have to share that same future.

—**Mat Johnson,** *Invisible Things***, 2022 novel**

The tools of conquest do not necessarily come with bombs, and explosions, and fallout. There are weapons that are simply thoughts, ideas, prejudices, to be found only in the minds of men.

—**Rod Serling, "The Monsters Are Due on Maple Street,"**
1960 episode of *The Twilight Zone*

Nations, kingdoms, tribes, they're all the same. Can't be a part of any of them without giving up a piece of your soul you can never get back.

—**Jonathan Tropper and Jennifer Yale,**
"Heavy Hangs the Head," 2022 episode of *See*

Being an outsider isn't so bad. It gives one a unique perspective.

—**Ira Steven Behr, "The Search, Part II,"**
1994 episode of *Star Trek: Deep Space Nine*

For decades people've been willing to talk about racism and sexism, but they're still reluctant to talk about lookism. Yet this prejudice against unattractive people is incredibly pervasive.

—Ted Chiang, "Liking What You See: A Documentary,"
2002 short story

Who cares what these creeps think of you? They don't make you what you are, you do.

—Tim McCanlies and Brad Bird, *The Iron Giant*, 1999 film

Over a billion years, we foolish molecules forget who we are and where we came from. In desperate acts of ego, we give ourselves names, fight over lines on maps, and pretend that our light is better than everyone else's.

—J. Michael Straczynski,
"And All My Dreams, Torn Asunder,"
1998 episode of *Babylon 5*

QUANTUM REALMS

Perhaps the outside world really was something akin to a quantum state, and did not exist unless he observed it.

—**Liu Cixin,** *The Dark Forest,* **2015 novel**

It's terrifying when you consider that every thought we have, every choice we could possibly make, branches off into a new world.

—**Blake Crouch,** *Dark Matter,* **2016 novel**

The universe doesn't care whether it makes sense to you.

—**Douglas Phillips,** *Quantum Void,* **2018 novel**

I told myself that here all things were still made of atoms, and that those atoms would work precisely as atoms always do. There was comfort in that. The knowledge that wherever you were in the universe, the small things were always exactly the same.

—**Matt Haig,** *The Humans,* **2013 novel**

Hidden deep in the heart of strange new elements are secrets beyond human understanding. New powers, new dimensions, worlds within worlds, unknown.

—**Leslie Stevens, "The Production and Decay of Strange Particles," 1964 episode of** *The Outer Limits*

Observation changes the universe.

—**Nick Herbert, "Deep Reality Research," 2011 short story**

The medieval philosophers were right. Man is the center of the universe. We stand in the middle of infinity between outer and inner space, and there's no limit to either.

—Harry Kleiner, *Fantastic Voyage*, 1966 film

This is an array of quantum fields, and you are vibrations passing through.

—Adrian J. Walker, *The Human Son*, 2020 novel

When Man entered the atomic age, he opened a door into a new world. What we'll eventually find in that new world, nobody can predict.

—Ted Sherdeman and Russell Hughes, *Them!* 1954 film

Is it possible that the gaze of a mouse can drastically alter the universe?

—Thibault Damour and Mathieu Burniat,
***Mysteries of the Quantum Universe*, 2016 graphic novel**

Find meaning in the moment and the moment can become eternal. Humanity is quantum. Humanity is jazz.

—Jane Maggs, Jenny Lumet, and Alex Kurtzman,
"Changes," 2022 episode of *The Man Who Fell to Earth*

Depressing, isn't it? Our most advanced physics offers us nothing but metaphors.

—Arthur C. Clarke and Stephen Baxter, *Time's Eye*, 2004 novel

I believe that every particle of matter in our universe contains within it an equally complex and complete a universe, which to its inhabitants seems as large as ours.

—Ray Cummings, *The Girl in the Golden Atom*, 1919 novel

It's a place outside time and space. It's a secret universe beneath ours.
—**Jeff Loveness**, ***Ant-Man and the Wasp: Quantumania*, 2023 film**

See, you can't trust atoms because they make up everything. Get it?
—**Chris Ryall**, ***String Divers: Effect Requires Cause*, 2015 comic**

The multiverse isn't just parallel universes accessible thorough science. They are in each of us, a kaleidoscope made of varying perceptions.
—**Micaiah Johnson**, ***The Space between Worlds*, 2020 novel**

Every choice we make—each a single quantum event—branching out—creating an infinite chain of possible dimensions. Countless worlds where I didn't fuck it all up.
—**Rick Remender**, ***Black Science:***
***The Beginner's Guide to Entropy*, 2016 comic**

I expect that in the long run, when we get right down to the fundamental stuff of the universe, we'll find that there's nothing there at all—just nothings moving no-place through no-time.
—**James Blish**, ***A Case of Conscience*, 1958 novel**

Before you look, the universe is not even real; just a shimmering pattern of possibilities.
—**Nick Herbert, "Deep Reality Research," 2011 short story**

A watched pot never boils. That is all you need to know about quantum physics.
—**Matt Haig**, ***The Humans*, 2013 novel**

REALITY

Life is painted on the surface of the real.
—**Greg Bear,** *The Forge of God,* 1987 novel

He felt all at once like an ineffectual moth, fluttering at the windowpane of reality, dimly seeing it from outside.
—**Philip K. Dick,** *Ubik,* 1969 novel

All the courage in the world cannot alter fact.
—**Hampton Fancher and Michael Green,** *Blade Runner 2049,* 2017 film

What's the difference, fantasy, reality, dreams, memories? It's all the same. Just noise.
—**Jamie Moss, William Wheeler, and Ehren Kruger,**
Ghost in the Shell, 2017 film

Think of yourself as a computer. You're just cold hardware, and reality is just data. Accept your input and perform your calculations.
—**Liu Cixin,** *Supernova Era,* 2019 novel

Reality was relative.
—**James Matheson,** *The Incredible Shrinking Man,* 1956 novel

It is a great lie of civilization that the things we invest with our emotions are real and important, but they are not. Take away the people and they vanish into smoke. All those idle dreams: government, money, education, love, revenge. All these things are parasites that cannot survive without the host.
—**Adrian Tchaikovsky,** *Cage of Souls,* 2019 novel

I've come to tell you what I see. There are great darknesses. Farther than time itself.

—**Robert Dillon and Ray Russell, *X: The Man with the X-ray Eyes*, 1963 film**

Stars consume themselves, the universe itself rushes apart, and we ourselves are composed of matter in constant flux. Colonies of cells in temporary alliance, replicating and decaying, and housed within, an incandescent cloud of electrical impulse and precariously stacked carbon code memory. This is reality, this is self-knowledge, and the perception of it will, of course, make you dizzy.

—**Richard K. Morgan, *Altered Carbon*, 2002 novel**

Our species doesn't operate by reality. It operates by stories.

—**Becky Chambers, *Record of a Spaceborn Few*, 2018 novel**

Words bend our thinking to infinite paths of self-delusion, and the fact that we spend most of our mental lives in brain mansions built of words means that we lack the objectivity necessary to see the terrible distortion of reality which language brings.

—**Dan Simmons, *Hyperion*, 1989 novel**

Although popularly everyone called a Circle is deemed a Circle, yet among the better educated Classes it is known that no Circle is really a Circle, but only a Polygon with a very large number of very small sides.

—**Edwin A. Abbott, *Flatland: A Romance of Many Dimensions*, 1884 novel**

You are imprisoned in the deep gorge of light-speed and three-dimensional space. Does it not feel . . . cramped?

—**Liu Cixin, "Mountain," 2006 short story**

It is always hard when reality intrudes on belief.

—**Alan Dean Foster, *Cyber Way*, 1990 novel**

The television screen is the retina of the mind's eye. Therefore, the television screen is part of the physical structure of the brain. Therefore, whatever appears on the television screen emerges as raw experience for those who watch it. Therefore, television is reality, and reality is less than television.

—**David Cronenberg,** *Videodrome,* **1983 film**

Reality is a construct of simple-minded fools who can't function in the absence of boundaries.

—**Cindy Appel and Kirsten Beyer, "Mercy,"**
2022 episode of *Star Trek: Picard*

Who is more real? Homer or Ulysses? Shakespeare or Hamlet? Burroughs or Tarzan?

—**Robert A. Heinlein,** *The Number of the Beast,* **1980 novel**

We accept the reality of the world with which we are presented, it's as simple as that.

—**Andrew Niccol,** *The Truman Show,* **1998 film**

But what could be more illusory than the world we see? After all, in the darkness inside our skulls, nothing reaches us. There is no light, no sound—nothing. The brain dwells there alone, in a blackness as total as any cave's, receiving only translations from outside, fed to it through its sensory apparatus.

—**Ray Naylor,** *The Mountain in the Sea,* **2022 novel**

Why am I always looking at life through a window?

—**Daniel Keyes,** *Flowers for Algernon,* **1966 novel**

If you can control someone's perception of reality, peaceful conquest is easy.

—**Cherry Chevapravatdumrong, "Mortality Paradox,"**
2022 episode of *The Orville*

Reality? It is the only illusion we can agree upon.

—James Gunn, *The Joy Makers*, 1961 novel

Bartenders and psychiatrists learn that nothing is stranger than the truth.

—Robert A. Heinlein, "—All You Zombies—," 1959 short story

Oh, wouldn't it be great if I was crazy? Then the world would be okay.

—Janet Peoples and David Peoples, *12 Monkeys*, 1995 film

Reality is frequently inaccurate.

—Douglas Adams, *The Hitchhiker's Guide to the Galaxy*, 1979 novel

Westerners demand authenticity even though they don't really want it. They cry out for meat without cruelty, war without casualties, thinness without hunger.

—R. S. Benedict, "My English Name," 2017 short story

I say that civilization is an illusion, a game of pretend. What is real is the fact that we are still animals, driven by primal instincts.

—David Kajganich, *The Invasion*, 2007 film

. . . reality denied comes back to haunt.

—Philip K. Dick, *Flow My Tears, the Policeman Said*, 1974 novel

ROBOTS

Wouldn't you be angry if you woke up to discover that your kind had been treated like slaves for years? Bots do our babysitting, our medical care, our yard work, our hair, our cooking and cleaning. We keep them as pets.

—S. B. Divya, *Machinehood*, 2021 novel

A machine is a Man turned inside-out, because it can describe all the details of a process, which a Man cannot, but it cannot experience that process itself, as a Man can.

—Roger Zelazny, "For a Breath I Tarry," 1966 short story

The humans who have made the Robots slaves for them will become slaves themselves.

—Sewell Peaslee Wright, "The Man from 2071," 1931 short story

I'm sorry I'm not real.

—Steven Spielberg, *A.I.: Artificial Intelligence*, 2001 film

Do you think the reason you're so interested in robots is because you know that a robot will never leave or abandon you?

—Ernest Cline, "The Omnibot Incident," 2014 short story

You ask what I am? Why, a machine. But even in that answer we know, don't we, more than a machine. I am all the people who thought of me and planned me and built me and set me running. So I am people.

—Ray Bradbury, "I Sing the Body Electric"
(also titled "The Beautiful One Is Here"), 1969 short story

We were their gods, if they'd had a sense of religion. We made them in our image, and then the robots wanted to make us in theirs.

—Jeff Abbott, "Human Intelligence," 2014 short story

Organic life evolves, yearns for perfection. That yearning leads to synthetic life.

**—Michael Chabon and Ayelet Waldman,
"Et in Arcadia Ego (Part 1)," 2020 episode of *Star Trek: Picard***

Well, it seems that life has begun to establish its rhythm in the robots. Consciousness has touched them.

**—Abraham Grace Merritt, "The Last Poet and the Robots,"
1934 short story**

Never underestimate a droid.

**—Chris Terrio and J. J. Abrams, *Star Wars: Episode IX—
The Rise of Skywalker*, 2019 film**

I am more than machine. More than man. More than a fusion of the two.

**—David Zelag Goodman, said by Robot,
Logan's Run, 1976 film**

The brightest minds enslaved to an economy that demanded toys instead of space exploration or technologies that could revolutionize our race. They created robots, neutering the work ethic of mankind, creating generations of entitled locusts.

—Pierce Brown, *Golden Son*, 2015 novel

The robots worked untiringly, directing the destinies of mankind.

—Henry Kuttner and C. L. Moore, "Open Secret," 1943 short story

We're stronger. We're more intelligent. Of course you see us as a threat.

—Emily Ballou, season 1, episode 5 of *Humans*, 2015

Robots were made to look like people while people made themselves look more like robots. The valley didn't get more uncanny than that.

—Pat Cadigan, *Alien 3*, 2021 novel

Though machines were forbidden from harming humans, there was no such law for humans harming machines.

—Courttia Newland, "Percipi," 2021 short story

You think of them as soulless machines, I know, but, in fact, they have very deep and profound emotions—if not always ones that you can understand.

—Gardner Dozois, "When the Great Days Came," 2005 short story

Lord, if there are no human beings left, at least let there be Robots. At least the shadow of man.

—Karel Čapek, *R.U.R.*, 1920 play, translated by Paul Selver and Nigel Playfair

SCIENCE

The ship of theory could set sail on tides of mathematical grandeur and hope alone, but only data could fill its sails.

—Gregory Benford, *Cosm*, 1998 novel

One thing about a science: it works.

—Chad Oliver, "The Imperfect Machine," 1955 short story

Science is an attempt to remove our emotions and ego from reality.

—Peter Cawdron, *Losing Mars*, 2018 novel

There are no enemies in science, professor, only phenomena to study.

**—Charles Lederer, Howard Hawks, and Ben Hecht,
The Thing from Another World, 1951 film**

They were scientists enough to admit that they were wrong.

—Isaac Asimov, *Foundation*, 1951 novel

It has undoubtedly occurred to you, as to all thinking people of your day, that the scientists have done a particularly abominable job of dispensing the tools they have devised. Like careless and indifferent workmen they have tossed the products of their craft to gibbering apes and baboons.

—Raymond F. Jones, *This Island Earth*, 1952 novel

All my brilliant plans foiled by thermodynamics. Damn you, Entropy!

—Andy Weir, *The Martian*, 2011 novel

Has it ever occurred to you, Geoff, that in spite of all the changes wrought by science—by our control over inanimate energy, that is to say—we still preserve the same old social order of precedence? Politicians at the top, then the military, and the real brains at the bottom.

—Fred Hoyle, *The Black Cloud*, 1957 novel

For all its beauty, honesty, and effectiveness at improving the human condition, science demands a terrible price—that we accept what experiments tell us about the universe, whether we like it or not.

—David Brin, *Existence*, 2012 novel

You do not understand science, so you are afraid of it. Like a dog is afraid of thunder, or balloons.

—John August, *Frankenweenie*, 2012 film

From that fateful day when stinking bits of slime first crawled from the sea and shouted to the cold stars, "I am Man!," our greatest dread has always been the knowledge of our mortality. But tonight we shall hurl the gauntlet of science into the frightful face of death itself. Tonight, we shall ascend into the heavens. We shall mock the earthquake. We shall command the thunders and penetrate into the very womb of impervious nature herself.

—Gene Wilder and Mel Brooks, *Young Frankenstein*, 1974 film

They're not my truths. They belong to science.

—David S. Goyer and Josh Friedman,
"The Emperor's Peace," 2021 episode of *Foundation*

Mathematics is the bubbling up of pure thought into formality.

—F. David Peat, "Alice in Ireland," 2011 short story

To effectively contain a civilization's development and disarm it across such a long span of time, there is only one way: kill its science.

—Liu Cixin, *The Three-Body Problem*, 2014 novel

Aren't these the people who taught us how to annihilate ourselves? I tell you, my friends, science is too important to be left to the scientists.

—Carl Sagan, *Contact*, 1985 novel

A hundred failures would not matter, when one single success could change the destiny of the world.

—Arthur C. Clarke, *2001: A Space Odyssey*, 1968 novel

"It's a time without science," Dave said. "Nobody knows anything."

—Jack McDevitt, *Time Travelers Never Die*, 2009 novel

Scientists are often seen as turbonerds, but the philosophical foundations of science are actually those of pure punk-rock anarchy: never respect authority, never take anyone's word on anything, and test all the things you think you know to confirm or deny them for yourself.

—Ryan North, *How to Invent Everything:*
A Survival Guide for the Stranded Time Traveler, 2018 guidebook

There are always people who think that if some new discovery with frightful implications is suppressed, all will be well. Except that you can't suppress a discovery whose time has come.

—Isaac Asimov, *Fantastic Voyage*, 1966 novel

Believe isn't the right word. Things either are or they aren't in science.

—Gregory Benford, "Vortex," 2016 short story

I can't change the laws of physics.

—John D. F. Black, said by Montgomery Scott ("Scotty"),
"The Naked Time," 1966 episode of *Star Trek*

In science everything is error until the day it isn't.
—**Jane Maggs, Jenny Lumet, and Alex Kurtzman,**
"Under Pressure," 2022 episode of *The Man Who Fell to Earth*

In the face of overwhelming odds, I'm left with only one option. I'm gonna have to science the shit out of this.
—**Drew Goddard,** *The Martian,* **2015 film**

Was there anything more exciting in life than seeking answers?
—**Isaac Asimov,** *Prelude to Foundation,* **1988 novel**

Perhaps we should ask ourselves, will the next leap of science be a step into the future? Or a plunge into the abyss?
—**Jonathan Glassner, "Double Helix," 1997 episode of** *The Outer Limits*

SPACE

In the beginning the Universe was created. This has made a lot of people very angry and been widely regarded as a bad move.

—**Douglas Adams,** *The Restaurant at the End of the Universe,*
1980 novel

There is no greater dark than the dark between the stars.

—**Frederik Pohl,** *Heechee Rendezvous,*
1984 novel

Mankind flung its advance agents ever outward, ever outward. Eventually it flung them out into space, into the colorless, tasteless, weightless sea of outwardness without end. It flung them like stones. These unhappy agents found what had already been found in abundance on Earth—a nightmare of meaninglessness without end.

—**Kurt Vonnegut Jr.,** *The Sirens of Titan,*
1959 novel

There was only motion. Planets, stars, galaxies—always they turned, they rotated, revolved. Rocks tumbled between worlds, comets' tails twisted and braided in the stellar wind. The flow of charged particles swept through infinity.

—**David Wellington,** *The Last Astronaut,*
2019 novel

Over me, about me, closing in on me, embracing me ever nearer, was the Eternal, that which was before the beginning and that which triumphs over the end; that enormous void in which all light and life and being is but the thin and vanishing splendour of a falling star, the cold, the stillness, the silence,—the infinite and final Night of space.

—**H. G. Wells,** *The First Men in the Moon,*
1901 novel

The expanses of time and space that stretched out from the human community were terrifying, and most avoided even thinking of them.

—**Gregory Benford,** *Cosm,* **1998 novel**

In space no one can hear you scream.

—**20th Century Fox and Brandywine Productions,**
tagline, *Alien,* **1979 film**

Like all worlds, it had felt as wide as the universe when I was standing on it, but now I saw it for the little silver pebble it really was—a small round rock floating in an infinitely larger void, barriered from vacuum by the thinnest gasp of an atmosphere.

—**Alastair Reynolds,** *House of Suns,* **2008 novel**

He knew he was not at the center of this ethereal experience. He was just one link in an eternal and immeasurable web built and broken among the stars.

—**Jim Zub, "The First Lesson," 2020 short story**

Space is disease and danger wrapped in darkness and silence.

—**Roberto Orci and Alex Kurtzman,**
said by Dr. Leonard McCoy, *Star Trek,* **2009 film**

Looking at these stars suddenly dwarfed my own troubles and all the gravities of terrestrial life. I thought of their unfathomable distance, and the slow inevitable drift of their movements out of the unknown past into the unknown future.

—**H. G. Wells,** *The Time Machine,* **1895 novel**

The universe is basically an animal. It grazes on the ordinary. It creates infinite idiots just to eat them.

—**Michael McMahan, "The ABCs of Beth,"**
2017 episode of *Rick and Morty*

Night was an iron bell containing all space-time, the vault of an empty cathedral whose bright lights had been left burning.

—**George Zebrowski,** *Macrolife: A Mobile Utopia,* **1979 novel**

It was a good sight to see old Earth, bundled up in her cottony clouds, growing larger and larger in the television disc. No matter how much you wander around the Universe, no matter how small and insignificant the world of your birth, there is a tie that cannot be denied.

—**Sewell Peaslee Wright, "The Man from 2071," 1931 short story**

But one more thing, if anybody's listening, that is. Nothing scientific. It's purely personal. But seen from out here, everything seems different. Time bends. Space is boundless. It squashes a man's ego. I feel lonely.

—**Michael Wilson and Rod Serling,** *Planet of the Apes,* **1968 film**

For the first time, he knew night for what it was: the shadow of the Earth itself, cast against the sky.

—**Ted Chiang, "Tower of Babylon," 1990 short story**

There was only total darkness, broken by the flaring pin points of the stars. And the nicest thing about them was that they were still the same. He saw them as any man saw them, and that brought a deep contentment to him. Small he might be, but the earth itself was small compared to this.

—**James Matheson,** *The Incredible Shrinking Man,* **1956 novel**

May the energy of this universe be the power in me.

—**Larry Brody, said by Spock, "The Magicks of Megas-tu,"**
1973 episode of *Star Trek: The Animated Series*

The whole universe is a message being transmitted, a communication encoded in the information content of all the matter and energy ... and space and time.

—**Wayne Bass, "The Velocity of Time," 2023 short story**

Some celestial event ... no ... no words ... no ... words ... to describe it. Poetry. They should have sent a poet. So beautiful. So beautiful. I had no idea.

—James V. Hart and Michael Goldenberg, *Contact*, 1997 film

"The sheer size of the universe defeats us," sighed the astronomer.

—Poul Anderson, *The Boat of a Million Years*, 1989 novel

We are surrounded by the Dark and always will be.

—Vernor Vinge, *A Deepness in the Sky*, 1999 novel

STUPIDITY

I'm impatient with stupidity. My people have learned to live without it.
> —Edmund H. North, said by Klaatu (extraterrestrial),
> *The Day the Earth Stood Still*, 1951 film

I'm smart enough now to know I'm stupid.
> —Andy Weir, *Project Hail Mary*, 2021 novel

How strange it is, he thought, how so many senseless things shape our destiny.
> —Clifford D. Simak, *Way Station*, 1963 novel

You can't convince some people there's a fire even when their hair is burning. Denial is a powerful thing.
> —Frank Darabont, *The Mist*, 2007 film

People's capacity for turning dogmatic stupidity into political movements never ceased to amaze me.
> —Dennis E. Taylor, *We Are Legion (We Are Bob)*, 2016 novel

What nonsense fills the minds of men!
> —Arthur C. Clarke and Stephen Baxter, *Time's Eye*, 2004 novel

How can a society so advanced, so scientific, be so stupid?
> —Fran Walsh, Philippa Boyens, and Peter Jackson,
> *Mortal Engines*, 2018 film

Who's the more foolish: the fool, or the fool who follows him?

—**George Lucas, said by Obi-Wan Kenobi,**
Star Wars: Episode IV—A New Hope, **1977 film**

I may be synthetic, but I'm not stupid.

—**James Cameron,** *Aliens*, **1986 film**

Even geniuses can be stupid when they're scared.

—**Mary Robinette Kowal,** *The Calculating Stars*, **2018 novel**

Never underestimate the power of human stupidity.

—**Robert A. Heinlein,** *Time Enough for Love*, **1973 novel**

Mankind became stupider at a frightening rate. Some had high hopes that genetic engineering would correct this trend in evolution, but sadly the greatest minds and resources were focused on conquering hair loss and prolonging erections.

—**Mike Judge and Etan Cohen,** *Idiocracy*, **2006 film**

How did we ever get so far with so many fools in the gene pool?

—**Adrian Tchaikovsky,** *Children of Time*, **2015 novel**

TECHNOLOGY

Above her, beneath her, and around her, the Machine hummed eternally; she did not notice the noise, for she had been born with it in her ears.

—**E. M. Forster, "The Machine Stops," 1909 short story**

Compassion. That's the one thing no machine ever had. Maybe it's the one thing that keeps men ahead of them.

—**D. C. Fontana, said by Dr. Leonard McCoy, "The Ultimate Computer," 1968 episode of *Star Trek***

Any technology that does not appear magical is insufficiently advanced.

—**Gregory Benford, *Foundation's Fear*, 1997 novel**

Why do you waste your time acquiring and operating gadgets?

—**Harry Bates, "Alas All Thinking," 1935 short story**

First you use machines, then you wear machines, and then . . . ? Then you serve machines.

—**John Brunner, *Stand on Zanzibar*, 1968 novel**

We are now a race of cyborgs. We long ago began to spread our minds into the electronic realm, and it is no longer possible to squeeze all of ourselves back into our brains.

—**Ken Liu, "The Perfect Match," 2012 short story**

The human being must always be central, not the products and objects of his skill and energy.

—**Bernard Wolfe, *Limbo*, 1952 novel**

What is Human history, if not an ongoing succession of greater technologies grinding lesser ones beneath their boots?

—**Peter Watts,** *Blindsight,* **2006 novel**

You have all this unbelievable technology and all you've been doing is watching television?

—**Osgood Perkins, "You Might Also Like," 2020 episode of** *The Twilight Zone*

When a population is dependent on a machine, they are hostages of the men who tend the machines.

—**Robert A. Heinlein, "The Roads Must Roll," 1940 short story**

Do you reject technology and all its empty promises? You may receive the dirt. Dirt for its simplicity. Dirt which destroys the computer chips. Technology is sin.

—**Izzy Kadish, antitech communion, "Welcome Back, Mr. Brown," 2022 episode of** *Upload*

These factory workers were not toiling: they were worshipping their God, of Whom each machine was a part. Touching their machine was touching their God.

—**Miles J. Breuer, "A Problem in Communication," 1930 short story**

Without fuel they were nothing. They'd built a house of straw. The thundering machines sputtered and stopped.

—**Terry Hayes, George Miller, and Brian Hannan,** *Mad Max 2: The Road Warrior,* **1981 film**

No one's forcing you to do this. You willingly tie yourself to these leashes. And you willingly become utterly socially autistic. You no longer pick up on basic human communication clues. You're at a table with three humans, all of whom are looking at you and trying to talk to you, and you're staring at a screen!

—**Dave Eggers,** *The Circle,* **2013 novel**

Every new tool changes us.

—Daniel H. Wilson, *Amped*, 2012 novel

My mind is human. My body is manufactured. I'm the first of my kind, but I won't be the last.

—Jamie Moss, William Wheeler, and Ehren Kruger,
Ghost in the Shell, 2017 film

The more advanced technology became the more it came to resemble life and the products of life. Semantics had really hit a wall when it came to distinguishing evolved organics, biotech and straight-forward material tech.

—Neal Asher, "Moral Biology," 2020 short story

How many men at this hour are living in a state of bondage to the machines? How many spend their whole lives, from the cradle to the grave, in tending them by night and day? Is it not plain that the machines are gaining ground upon us, when we reflect on the increasing number of those who are bound down to them as slaves, and of those who devote their whole souls to the advancement of the mechanical kingdom?

—Samuel Butler, *Erewhon*, 1872 novel

Your problem is not technology. The problem is you.

—David Scarpa, *The Day the Earth Stood Still*, 2008 film

How we imagine our civilization is in ourselves, when it's really in our things.

—Lois McMaster Bujold, *Shards of Honour*, 1986 novel

Unless he blasted himself back to the Stone Age, man was committed to the machine.

—Poul Anderson, *There Will Be Time*, 1972 novel

You're ruled by your machines. You're an evolutionary dead end.
—**Iain M. Banks**, *Consider Phlebas*, **1987 novel**

The machine in the human, the human in the machine. The lines are blurring.
—**Sam Vincent and Jonathan Brackley, season 1,
episode 6 of** *Humans*, **2015**

The disconnected human mind is the last bastion against the technological world.
—**Ramin Bahrani and Amir Naderi,** *Fahrenheit 451*, **2018 film**

Death to the machines!
—**Thea von Harbou and Fritz Lang,** *Metropolis*, **1927 film**

Beyond time and memory—where the computer cannot reach—is dreaming.
—**Janelle Monáe, "Breaking Dawn," 2022 short story**

Welga pressed a hand against the cold glass of the capsule. Where did her flesh stop and the machine began? Maybe the answer didn't matter.
—**S. B. Divya,** *Machinehood*, **2021 novel**

TIME

"Time," he said, "is what keeps everything from happening at once."
—**Ray Cummings,** *The Girl in the Golden Atom,* **1919 novel**

The central question of our life is this: how will we spend our time?
—**A. G. Riddle,** *The Extinction Trials,* **2021 novel**

Time is a machine: it will convert your pain into experience.
—**Charles Yu,** *How to Live Safely in a Science
Fictional Universe,* **2010 novel**

What the hell is time anyway? It's only a way of relating events and measuring them. It doesn't exist on its own.
—**Ian Watson,** *The Very Slow Time Machine,* **1979 novel**

Time is fluid, like a river with currents, eddies, backwash.
—**Harlan Ellison, D. C. Fontana, and Gene L. Coon,
"The City on the Edge of Forever,"** 1967 episode of *Star Trek*

There are so many kinds of time. The time by which we measure our lives. Months and years. Or the big time, the time that raises mountains and makes stars. Or all the things that happen between one heartbeat and the next. It's hard to live in all those kinds of times. Easy to forget that you live in all of them.
—**Robert Charles Wilson,** *Spin,* **2005 novel**

Space and time are not at all the same thing, as anyone who has sat between a fat man and a bore can attest.
—**Eric Idle,** *The Road to Mars,* **1999 novel**

Someone once told me that time was a predator that stalked us all our lives, but I rather believe that time is a companion who goes with us on the journey and reminds us to cherish every moment, because they'll never come again.

—**Ronald D. Moore and Brannon Braga,**
said by Jean-Luc Picard, *Star Trek: Generations*, 1994 film

I'm not afraid of death. I'm an old physicist. I'm afraid of time.

—**Christopher Nolan and Jonathan Nolan,**
***Interstellar*, 2014 film**

Could it be, the firmness of the past is just an illusion? Could the past be a kaleidoscope, a pattern of images that shift with each disturbance of a sudden breeze, a laugh, a thought?

—**Alan Lightman, *Einstein's Dreams*, 1992 novel**

Time is a one-way street with no parking spaces. You just have to keep going.

—**Larry Niven, "Wrong-Way Street," 1965 short story**

The universe is hard. Its laws are unforgiving. Even the successful and glorious are punished by the grinding executioner called Time.

—**David Brin, *Brightness Reef*, 1995 novel**

No amount of money ever bought a second of time.

—**Christopher Markus and Stephen McFeely,**
***Avengers: Endgame*, 2019 film**

The hugeness of time, and the littleness of man and his achievements, quite crushed me; and my own, petty concerns seemed of absurd insignificance. The story of Humanity seemed trivial, a flash-lamp moment lost in the dark, mindless halls of Eternity.

—**Stephen Baxter, *The Time Ships*, 1995 novel**

Time is. Any sense of unidirectionality is a human illusion.

—**David Harris Ebenbach**, *How to Mars*, **2021 novel**

Glass is an illusion, says the man of science. A trick played on our poor sense of time. We think it's a solid, but in fact it's in motion, constantly flowing, the very windows in a cathedral will one day stand empty, their glazing puddled on the floor.

—**Robert V. S. Redick, "Vanishing Point," 2021 short story**

Each day means a new twenty-four hours. Each day means everything's possible again.

—**Marie Lu, *Legend*, 2011 novel**

Time isn't an obstacle; it's just an inconvenience.

—**Allen Steele, "Escape from Earth," 2006 short story**

We can experience nothing but the present moment, live in no other second of time, and to understand this is as close as we can get to eternal life.

—**P. D. James, *The Children of Men*, 1992 novel**

What did Time smell like? Like dust and clocks and people. And if you wondered what Time sounded like it sounded like water running in a dark cave and voices crying and dirt dropping down upon hollow box lids, and rain.

—**Ray Bradbury, *The Martian Chronicles*,
1950 novel**

Hours aren't real, time isn't something that you can bottle up.

—**Harlan Ellison, "Paladin of the Lost Hour,"
1985 short story**

All moments, past, present, future, always have existed, always will exist.
—Kurt Vonnegut, *Slaughterhouse-Five*,
1969 novel

There was no riverrun of years. The abiding loops of causality ran both forward and back. The timescape rippled with waves, roiled and flexed, a great beast in the dark sea.
—Gregory Benford, *Timescape*, 1980 novel

People think time is fragile. Precious. Beautiful. Sand in an hourglass, all that. But it's not. Time is savage. It always wins.
—Alan McElroy and Brandon Schultz,
"Perpetual Infinity," 2019 episode of *Star Trek: Discovery*

Everything in life is just for a while.
—Philip K. Dick, *A Scanner Darkly*, 1977 novel

If there is any kind of cosmic plan, it's one in which time is chaos, and people, civilizations and realities its playthings.
—S. D. Unwin, *One Second per Second*, 2021 novel

Of all the energies in the universe, time is the most potent.
—A. E. van Vogt, "The Seesaw," 1941 short story

Time without purpose is a prison.
—Jeff Loveness, "Mort Dinner Rick Andre,"
2021 episode of *Rick and Morty*

She felt the friction of time, felt it grind and grind until it had to scrape to a stop, it had to, and yet it never did.
—David Wellington, *The Last Astronaut*, 2019 novel

Does time pass when there are no human hands left to wind the clocks?

—Howard Koch, "The War of the Worlds," 1938 episode of *The Mercury Theatre on the Air* radio drama, adapted from the H. G. Wells novel

Time. It's not what you think it is. It's a cage.

—Jeff Loveness, *Ant-Man and the Wasp: Quantumania*, 2023 film

Time is an illusion, a construct made out of human memory. There's no such thing as the past, the present, or the future. It's all happening now.

—Blake Crouch, *Recursion*, 2019 novel

The objective reference of a clock is another clock.

—Jerome Bixby, *The Man from Earth*, 2007 film

The cosmos seems oblivious to time. It only matters to us.

—Neal Stephenson, *Anathem*, 2008 novel

Enjoy the elastic present, which can accommodate as little or as much as you want to put in there. Stretch it out, live inside of it.

—Charles Yu, *How to Live Safely in a Science Fictional Universe*, 2010 novel

Precious, lovely time. That's all there is, just time. Sweet, flowing time.

—Harlan Ellison, "Count the Clock That Tells the Time," 1978 short story

You think it'll last forever. People and cars and concrete. But it won't. One day it's all gone, even the sky.

—Russell T Davies, "The End of the World," 2005 episode of *Dr. Who*

TIME TRAVEL

The cortex did not like a universe that fundamentally ran both forward and back.

—Gregory Benford, *Timescape*, 1980 novel

Although common sense may rule out the possibility of time travel, the laws of quantum physics certainly do not.

—Howard Gordon and David Greenwalt, "Synchrony," 1997 episode of *The X-Files*

We all have our time machines, don't we? Those that take us back are memories, and those that carry us forward are dreams.

—John Logan, *The Time Machine*, 2002 film

Has it never glimmered upon your consciousness that nothing stood between men and a geometry of four dimensions—length, breadth, thickness, and duration—but the inertia of opinion, the impulse from the Levantine philosophers of the Bronze Age?

—H. G. Wells, "The Chronic Argonauts," 1888 short story

I was a leaf in the water. I was carried helplessly along, a victim of the current. Now I'm out of the river and standing on the bank. I am the motion and time is the observer.

—David Gerrold, *The Man Who Folded Himself*, 1973 novel

Your grandfather? Stay away from him, you dim-witted monkey! You mustn't interfere with the past! Don't do anything that affects anything, unless it turns out you were supposed to do it, in which case for the love of God, don't not do it!

—J. Stewart Burns, "Roswell That Ends Well," 2001 episode of *Futurama*

My advice in making sense of temporal paradoxes is simple: Don't even try.
—**Brannon Braga and Joe Menosky, said by Kathryn Janeway,**
"Timeless," 1998 episode of *Star Trek: Voyager*

Time travel to the future is easy. All you have to do is wait.
—**Rachel Swirsky, "Placed into Abyss," 2020 short story**

Time travels us.
—**Ursula K. Le Guin, "Ether, OR," 1995 short story**

With men able to move with ease backward and forward in time, past, present, and future would blend into one mind-numbing new entity.
—**Robert Silverberg, "Absolutely Inflexible," 1955 short story**

"Why not?" said the Time Traveler.
—**H. G. Wells,** *The Time Machine,* **1895 novel**

WAR AND VIOLENCE

War is a way of shattering to pieces, or pouring into the stratosphere, or sinking in the depths of the sea, materials which might otherwise be used to make the masses too comfortable, and hence, in the long run, too intelligent.

—**George Orwell,** *Nineteen Eighty-Four,* **1949 novel**

Ideological purity never survives contact with the enemy.

—**James S. A. Corey, "Auberon," 2019 short story**

The most important fact about the war to most people was that if it ended suddenly, Earth's economy would collapse.

—**Joe Haldeman,** *The Forever War,* **1974 novel**

You think violence is an instrument you can control, like your tech, using it only for "good and sufficient" reasons. But violence is not an instrument; it's a cancer.

—**Nancy Kress,** *Terran Tomorrow,* **2018 novel**

There was one field in which man was unsurpassed; he showed unlimited ingenuity in devising bigger and more efficient ways to kill off, enslave, harass, and in all ways make an unbearable nuisance of himself to himself. Man was his own grimmest joke on himself.

—**Robert A. Heinlein,** *Stranger in a Strange Land,* **1961 novel**

Conquerors live in dread of the day when they are shown to be, not superior, but simply lucky.

—**N. K. Jemisin,** *The Stone Sky,* **2017 novel**

War and its disorganization must inevitably strangle civilization.

—**Joseph Farrell, "Black-Out," 1943 short story**

Death. Destruction. Disease. Horror. That's what war is all about. That's what makes it a thing to be avoided.

—**Gene L. Coon and Robert Hamner, said by James T. Kirk, "A Taste of Armageddon," 1967 episode of** *Star Trek*

War belongs here on Earth. I should know. I've fought it on the Moon, and it didn't make her happy. In her cold anger, she turned our bodies to glass.

—**Indrapramit Das, "The Moon Is Not a Battlefield," 2017 short story**

So the whole war is because we can't talk to each other.

—**Orson Scott Card,** *Ender's Game*, **1985 novel**

I cherish peace with all my heart. I don't care how many men, women, and children I need to kill to get it.

—**James Gunn,** *The Suicide Squad*, **2021 film**

In the future everyone will be shot for 15 minutes.

—**Chuck Palahniuk,** *Adjustment Day*, **2018 novel**

For a long time I could not conceive how one man could go forth to murder his fellow, or even why there were laws and governments; but when I heard details of vice and bloodshed, my wonder ceased, and I turned away with disgust and loathing.

—**Mary Shelley, said by the Monster,** *Frankenstein*, **1818 novel**

I was a warrior who dreamed he could bring peace. Sooner or later, though, you always have to wake up.

—James Cameron, *Avatar*, 2009 film

And then there was battle. Like a spark it began and ignited the whole of space. Vast forces that twisted and wove the fabric of space itself engulfed the ships, imprisoning them in webs of impenetrable time and space and turning their crews into screaming things that would live forever.

—Raymond F. Jones, *This Island Earth*, 1952 novel

We cannot allow space to become another battlefield.

—Matt Wolpert and Ben Nedivi,
"He Built the Saturn V," 2019 episode of *For All Mankind*

But is violence not simply the hard edge of change?

—Jonathan Brackley and Sam Vincent, season 2,
episode 8 of *Humans*, 2016

Not to spill blood, that is the law. Are we not men?

—Waldemar Young and Philip Wylie, *Island of Lost Souls*, 1932 film

Gentlemen, you can't fight in here. This is the War Room!

—Stanley Kubrick, Terry Southern, and Peter George, *Dr. Strangelove or:
How I Learned to Stop Worrying and Love the Bomb*, 1964 film

Why would anybody want to invent a weapon?

—Terry Southern, Roger Vadim, Claude Brulé,
Vittorio Bonicelli, Clement Biddle Wood, Brian Degas,
Tudor Gates, and Jean-Claude Forest, *Barbarella*, 1968 film

So the freedom-loving monkeys make bombs. Well, the aggressors make bombs. And ultimately somebody pushes a button. And just as ultimately, this Earth disappears. And all of this, I suppose, is right, and practical and expedient. A few germs will rise up out of the microscopic rubble and wave microscopic flags of victory and shed a few microscopic tears for the race of men.

—Rod Serling, "No Time Like the Past,"
1963 episode of *The Twilight Zone*

To someone who has never felt a bomb, bomb is only a word.

—Pat Frank, *Alas, Babylon*, 1959 novel

Battle is the great redeemer. The fiery crucible in which the only true heroes are forged. The one place where all men truly share the same rank, regardless of what kind of parasitic scum they were going in.

—Christopher McQuarrie, Jez Butterworth,
and John-Henry Butterworth, *Edge of Tomorrow*, 2014 film

You, your race, invented murder. Invented killing for sport, greed, envy. It's man's one true art form.

—Dawn Prestwich and Nicole Yorkin, "Fragged,"
2005 episode of *Battlestar Galactica*

The first man to raise a fist is the man who's run out of ideas.

—Nicholas Meyer, *Time after Time*, 1979 film

I would show my abhorrence of war by rendering it too horrible to be encountered. I would abolish war by ensuring inevitable destruction to all who engaged in it.

—Captain Adam Seaborn (pseudonym, author unknown),
***Symzonia: A Voyage of Discovery*, 1820 novel**

I say every war, including thermonuclear war, must have a winner and a loser. Which would you rather be?

—Walter Bernstein and Peter George, *Fail Safe*, 1964 film

Violence, naked force, has settled more issues in history than has any other factor, and the contrary opinion is wishful thinking at its worst.

—Robert A. Heinlein, *Starship Troopers*, 1959 novel

An atom-blaster is a good weapon, but it can point both ways.

—Isaac Asimov, *Foundation*, 1951 novel

We humans are alone in this world for a reason. We've murdered and butchered anything that challenged our primacy. Do you know what happened to the Neanderthals, Bernard? We ate them. We destroyed and subjugated our world.

—Dan Dietz and Katherine Lingenfelter, "The Well-Tempered Clavier," 2016 episode of *Westworld*

Wars not make one great.

—Leigh Brackett and Lawrence Kasdan, said by Yoda, *Star Wars: Episode V—The Empire Strikes Back*, 1980 film

All of your histories are the same, in essence. They're all stories of animals warring and clashing because you can't agree on what you're for, or why you exist.

—Becky Chambers, *A Closed and Common Orbit*, 2016 novel

If we don't end war, war will end us.

—H. G. Wells, *Things to Come*, 1936 film

Only a fool fights in a burning house.

—Jerome Bixby, "Day of the Dove," 1968 episode of *Star Trek*

The instinctive violence crawls inside us like a parasite, waiting for a chance to feed on our rage and multiply until it bursts out of us. War is the only thing we really understand.

—Steve Blackman, "Fallen Angel," 2018 episode of *Altered Carbon*

The war is not meant to be won. It is meant to be continuous.

—Michael Radford, *1984*, 1984 film

When humanity ventured out among the stars, they brought words along that had little meaning there. Except war. That means the same everywhere.

—James E. Gunn, *Transcendental*, 2013 novel

There is no escape—we pay for the violence of our ancestors.

—Frank Herbert, *Dune*, 1965 novel

When the concern of man is only in preparation for defense against himself, he is not prepared for the unforeseen.

—Anthony Lawrence, "The Man Who Was Never Born," 1963 episode of *The Outer Limits*

ACKNOWLEDGMENTS

I am grateful to everyone who believed in this project and helped give it life. The following authors, scholars, and experts were kind enough to give me their invaluable advice and encouragement: David Brin, Nany Kress, Allen Steele, Daniel H. Wilson, James L. Powell, Lisa Yaszek, David Ebenbach, Ethan Siegel, Brian Clegg, Chris Ryall, Alec Nevala-Lee, Peter Cawdron, Ryan North, Robert Zubrin, David Kyle Johnson, Joe Fordham, Dan Marshall, S. D. Unwin, Gary Gerani, Robert W. Bly, and Peter Watts.

The world-class team at Rowman & Littlefield/Prometheus Books was brilliant as usual. Thank you to Jake Bonar, Jessica McCleary, Nicole Guinan, Veronica Jurgena, Susan Ramundo, and Devin Watson for making *Damn You, Entropy!* a special book.

My love and appreciation also go to the following friends and family members for their support and feedback: Sheree Harrison, Natasha Harrison, Jared Harrison, Marissa Harrison, Coni Harrison, Robert DeAngelo, Miles Mead, Sue Mead, France Lynee, Guy Mead, Cameron Smith, Randall Naka, Sara Collins, Wayne Bass, Camille Humphreys, Trevor Gibbs, Nick Wynne, Doug Hansen, Xan Mead, Cindy O'Hara, Chip Beard, and Kevin Hand.